Eulogies III

Edited by Christopher Jones
Nanci Kalanta
Tony Tremblay

HW Press

ೞ 2015 ೞ

Cover art © 2015 Deena Warner
Interior Art © 2014 Keith Minnion
Interior Layout by Nanci Kalanta
ISBN-10 0979234670
ISBN-13 9780979234675

HW Press
Website: www.hwpress.net

Acknowledgements

After the success of Eulogies II it didn't take much convincing for us to go forward with Eulogies III. Putting an anthology together is hard work but it helps when you have genuine respect for each other's vision and a common goal. Our goal is to make Eulogies a truly great anthology series.

Early on in the process we agreed we wanted Eulogies III to feature authors that had not appeared in Eulogies II and to represent a "wish list" of sorts.

Each of us submitted a list of authors that we wanted to see in Eulogies III and extended invitations to those authors. We were pleased that they all accepted.

The return of Deena Warner as the cover artist, and Keith Minnion as the interior artist insured that the anthology would continue the benchmark of quality set by Eulogies I and II. Both artists have become an integral part of the series.

We also have to thank Robert Dunbar, for writing the introduction. He was the unanimous choice to kick off the anthology and he nailed the introduction, conveying his deep respect and passion for the horror genre while touching on each story contained within.

Finally, Gary Braunbeck is an author we have all admired and respected for years and his amazing cover blurb was the bow that tied everything together.

You hold in your hands the culmination of a year's worth of blood, sweat and tears from the authors, the artists, and the editors. Here's hoping you're as pleased with Eulogies III as we are.

The editors would like to thank all of the contributors to Eulogies III. When it comes down to it, it's really their book. Special thanks to David Dodd for his help in making sure we didn't miss anything.

Christopher Jones

First and foremost, thanks to my partners Nanci and Tony. I truly feel blessed to know you guys. Thanks to my wife for her support throughout this venture. Also, special thanks to Janet Holden for her wisdom and encouragement. I would like to dedicate this book to my Dad, who had Straub and King on the bookshelf when I was growing up.

Nanci Kalanta

I would like to thank my husband for his support; Christopher, and Tony for their patience, and willingness to be open to new ideas, Keith Minnion for his remarkable interior artwork, his advice, and counsel; it is always good to learn from the best, and Deena Warner for her amazing artwork.

I would also like to thank Richard Chizmar, Don Koish, Kealan Patrick Burke, and Thomas Monteleone who, back when I started this journey in 2006 with the first Eulogies, took the time to share their advice and experience. They helped make Eulogies a success and continue to support HW Press to this day.

Tony Tremblay

I would like to acknowledge my wife Paula, son Anthony, daughter Laura, immediate family, and extended family for their support. I owe nods to Scott Goudsward and Stacey Longo, whose friendship and advice on anthologies is always welcomed. That nod also extends to the members of the NEHW who are always willing to share a discussion and table space. Kudo's also to my writers group, The Blank Page, who meet at the Goffstown Public Library, they are a constant reminder of the work and rewards in writing fiction. Tip of the hat to The Taco Society, their meetings keep it real by bringing it all down to earth.

Finally, I would like to thank Nanci Kalanta and Chris Jones, they are two of the finest people I have ever met. I consider it an honor that they call me friend.

Introduction
Robert Dunbar

"You must not forget that a monster is only a variation,
and that to a monster the norm is monstrous."
~ *John Steinbeck*

It can get a little hoary. The coffin creaking open.
The cobwebs. The bats. The misshapen thing howling on
the moors. Through overuse, the edge grows blunt. But
not around here. In the pages of EULOGIES III, horror is
still sharp as an axe.

Of course, it began on a promising note. The first
two *Eulogies* anthologies included the works of genre
luminaries like Gary Braunbeck, Kealan Patrick Burke,
Rick Hautala, James A. Moore, Tom Piccirilli, and Simon
Wood, among many others, and in just a few years, the
series has evolved into this extraordinary volume.
Nothing so commonplace as a werewolf or zombie lurks
within these pages. No, on offer here is an altogether
more complex assortment of evils… and a sampling of
humans who battle, retreat, suffer and are changed.
Orchestration accounts for a great deal of the
effectiveness, and the editors are to be congratulated on
the arrangement of these tales. It becomes a symphony of
horrors.

The opening chord is struck by David Morrell's *The Storm*. Lightning may fracture the sky, but a whip crack of devilish humor still resounds. This leads into the sulfurous fantasy of *Mr. Mumblety-Peg* by Tim Curran, followed by the savage wit of Violet LeVoit's *Terms and Conditions*.

Thomas Sullivan's sophisticated prose propels the rhythm and cadences of *Hate Me Afire*. (Sometimes evil is a passive thing, a mere lump of malignity. Sometimes it hunts for victims.) Next, *The Mouth* by Ray Garton yawns wide to reveal further depths of dread. Then the lyrically hypnotic terrors of Gemma Files' *In Hell, An Eye* offer a glimpse of the abyss. Demonology has its appeal. But angels may be more terrifying still. Never doubt it.

Bracken MacLeod manifests edgy irreverence in *Morgenstern's Last Act*, a brisk tale with noir shadings. The tone quickly alters: lost love and impossible longing can result in utter destruction, as revealed in Matt Moore's *One Last Drop Of Blood To Remember Me By*. Meanwhile, Elizabeth Massie's particular genius frays the nerves almost from the first words of *Fly Away Home*, a dark fable spun around an American icon and a historical horror.

With his customary verve, John Everson provides a child's view of emotional brutality in *The Hole to China*. Then Chet Williamson drags the reader – kicking and screaming – to the opposite end of the spectrum with the charnel house of *She Sits and Smiles*. The fetid shocks of *Carry On, Carrion* by Paula D. Ashe would have proved sufficiently intense to climax the anthology. But one more terror lurks.

The blade falls. Sly, vicious, and ultimately metaphysical, Brian Hodge's *One Possible Shape Of Things To Come* evokes a particularly unpleasant corner of hell on earth. Some shadowy places are more terrible than others. Who knows what might spring forth?

> "The artist must bow to the monster of his own imagination."
> ~ *Richard Wright*

When it comes to horror, contemporary readers labor under a great disadvantage: they are not easily frightened. But the world still has need of monsters. Abominations of all description fueled the ancient myths. Horrors lurk in religious texts… and in so many great works of world literature. Mankind cannot long survive without its nightmares. Nor should it. The dark tradition may boast venerable antecedents, but – as these authors demonstrate – its future remains secure. Don't be lulled by the title. **Eulogies III** boasts none of the grave's solemn stillness. It is a cauldron. It bubbles and hisses. All the ingredients of horror roil within. Savor the brew.

~ *Robert Dunbar*

The Storm
David Morrell

Gail saw it first. She came from the Howard Johnson's toward the heat haze in the parking lot where our son, Jeff, and I were hefting luggage into our station wagon. Actually, Jeff supervised. He gave me his excited ten-year-old advice about the best place for this suitcase and that knapsack. Grinning at his sun-bleached hair and nut-brown freckled face, I told him I could never have done the job without him.

It was eight a.m., Tuesday, August second, but even that early, the thermometer outside our motel unit had risen to eighty-five. The humidity was thick and smothering. Just from my slight exertion with the luggage, I'd sweated through my shirt and jeans, wishing I'd thought to put on shorts. To the east, the sun blazed, white and swollen, the sky an oppressive chalky blue. This would be one day when the station wagon's air-conditioning wouldn't be just a comfort but a necessity.

My hands were sweat-slick as I shut the hatch. Jeff nodded, satisfied with my work, then grinned beyond me. Turning, I saw Gail coming toward us. When she left the brown parched grass, her brow creased as her sandals touched the heat-softened asphalt parking lot.

All set?" she asked.

Her smooth white shorts and cool blue top emphasized her tan. She looked trim and lithe and wonderful. I'm not sure how she did it, but she seemed completely unaffected by the heat. Her hair was soft and golden. Her subtle trace of makeup made the day seem somehow cooler.

"Ready. Thanks to Jeff," I told her.

Jeff grinned up proudly.

"Well, I paid the bill. I gave them back the key," Gail said. "Let's go." She paused. "Except..."

"What's wrong?"

"Those clouds." She pointed past my shoulder.

I turned.

And frowned. In contrast with the blinding, chalky eastern sky, I stared at numbing, pitch-black western clouds. They seethed on the far horizon, roiling, churning. Lightning flickered like a string of flashbulbs in the distance, the thunder rumbling hollowly.

"Now where the hell did *that* come from?" I said. "It wasn't there before I packed the car."

Gail squinted toward the thunderheads. "You think we should wait till it passes?"

"It isn't close." I shrugged.

"But it's coming fast." Gail bit her lip. "And it looks bad."

Jeff grabbed my hand. I glanced at his worried face.

"It's just a storm, son."

Jeff surprised me, though. I'd misjudged what worried him.

"I want to go back home," he said. "I don't want to wait. I miss my friends. Please, can't we leave?"

I nodded. "I'm on your side. Two votes out of three, Gail. If you're really scared, though..."

"No. I..." Gail drew a breath and shook her head. "I'm being silly. It's just the thunder. You know how

18

storms bother me." She ruffled Jeff's hair. "But I won't
make us wait. I'm homesick, too."

We'd spent the past two weeks in Colorado, fishing,
camping, touring ghost towns. The vacation had been
perfect. But as eagerly as we'd gone, we were just as
eager to be heading back. Last night, we'd stopped here
in North Platte, a small quiet town off Interstate 80,
halfway through Nebraska. Now, today, we hoped we
could reach home in Iowa City by nightfall.

"Let's get moving then," I said. "It's probably a local
storm. We'll drive ahead of it. We'll never see a drop of
rain."

Gail tried to smile. "I hope."

Jeff hummed as we got in the station wagon. I
steered toward the interstate, went up the eastbound
ramp, and set the cruise control for the speed limit of
fifty-five. Ahead, the morning sun glared through the
windshield. After I tugged down the visors, I turned on
the air conditioner, then the radio. The local weatherman
said hot and hazy.

"Hear that?" I said. "He didn't mention a storm. No
need to worry. Those are only heat clouds."

* * *

I was wrong. From time to time, I checked the
rearview mirror, and the clouds loomed thicker, blacker,
closer, seething toward us down the interstate. Ahead,
the sun kept blazing fiercely. Jeff wiped his sweaty face. I
set the air conditioner for desert, but it didn't seem to
help.

"Jeff, reach in the ice chest. Grab us each a Coke."

He grinned. But I suddenly felt uneasy, realizing too
late that he'd have to turn to open the chest in the rear
compartment.

"Gosh," he murmured, staring back, awestruck.

19

"What's the matter?" Gail swung around before I could stop her. "Oh my God, the clouds."

They were angry midnight chasing us. Lightning flashed. Thunder jolted.

"They still haven't reached us," I said. "If you want, I'll try outrunning them."

"Do *something*."

I switched off the cruise control and sped to sixty, then sixty-five. The strain of squinting toward the white-hot sky ahead of us gave me a piercing headache. I put on my sunglasses.

But all at once I didn't need them. Abruptly the clouds caught up to us. The sky went totally black. We drove in roiling darkness.

"Seventy. I'm doing seventy," I said. "But the clouds are moving faster."

"Almost a hurricane," Gail said. "That isn't possible. Not in Nebraska."

"I'm scared," Jeff said.

He wasn't the only one. Lightning blinded me, stabbing to the right and left of us. Thunder shook the car. Then the air became an eerie dirty shade of green, and I started thinking about tornadoes.

"Find a place to stop!" Gail shouted.

But there wasn't one. We'd already passed the exit for the next town, Kearny. I searched for a roadside park, but a sign said REST STOP, THIRTY MILES. I couldn't just pull off the highway. On the shoulder, if the rain obscured another driver's vision, we could all be hit and killed. No choice. I had to keep on driving.

"At least it isn't raining," I said.

The clouds unloaded. No preliminary sprinkle. Massive raindrops burst around us, gusting, roaring, pelting.

"I can't see!" I flicked the windshield wipers to their highest setting. They flapped in sharp, staccato triple time. I peered through murky, undulating, windswept waves of water, struggling for a clear view of the highway.

I was going too fast. When I braked, the station wagon fishtailed. We skidded on the slippery pavement. I couldn't breathe. The tires gripped. I felt the jolt. Then the car was in control.

I slowed to forty, but the rain heaved with such force against the windshield I still couldn't see.

"Pull your seat belts tight."

* * *

Although I never found that rest stop, I got lucky when a flash of lightning showed a sign, the exit for a town called Grand Island. Shaking from tension, I eased down the off-ramp. At the bottom, across from me, a Best Western motel was shrouded with rain. We left a wake through the flooded parking lot and stopped under the motel's canopy. My hands were stiff from clenching the steering wheel. My shoulders ached. My eyes felt swollen, raw.

Gail and Jeff got out, rain gusting under the canopy as they ran inside. I had to move the car to park it in the lot. I locked the doors, but although I sprinted, I was drenched and chilled when I reached the motel's entrance.

Inside, a small group stared past me toward the storm — two clerks, two waitresses, a cleaning lady. I shook.

"Mister, use this towel," the cleaning lady said. She took one from a pile on her cart.

I thanked her, wiping my dripping face and soggy hair.

"See any accidents?" a waitress asked.

With the towel around my neck, I shook my head no.

"A storm this sudden, there ought to be accidents," the waitress said as if doubting me.

I frowned when she said *sudden*. "You mean it's just starting here?"

A skinny clerk stepped past me to the window. "Not too long before you came. A minute maybe. I looked out this window, and the sky was bright. I knelt to tie my shoe. When I stood up, the clouds were here — as black as night. I don't know where they came from all of a sudden, but I never saw it rain so hard so fast."

"But — " I shivered, puzzled. "The storm hit us back near Kearny. We've been driving in it for an hour."

"You were on the edge of it, I guess," the clerk said, spellbound by the devastation outside. "It followed you."

My cold wet shirt clung to me, but I felt a deeper chill.

"Looks like we've got other customers," the second clerk said, pointing out the window.

More cars splashed through the torrent in the parking lot.

"Yeah, we'll be busy, that's for sure," the clerk said. He switched on the lights, but they didn't dispel the outside gloom.

The wind howled.

I glanced around the lobby, suddenly noticing that Gail and Jeff weren't in sight. "My wife and son."

"They're in the restaurant," the second waitress said, smiling to reassure me. "Through that arch. They ordered coffee for you. Hot and strong."

"I need it. Thanks."

Dripping travelers stumbled in.

* * *

We waited an hour. Although the coffee was as hot as promised, it didn't warm me. In the air-conditioning, my soggy clothes stuck to the chilly chrome-and-plastic seat. A bone-deep freezing numbness made me sneeze.

"You need dry clothes," Gail said. "You'll catch pneumonia."

I'd hoped the storm would stop before I went out for the clothes. But even in the restaurant, I felt the thunder rumble. I couldn't wait. My muscles cramped from shivering. "I'll get a suitcase." I stood.

"Dad, be careful." Jeff looked worried.

Smiling, I leaned down and kissed him. "Son, I promise."

Near the restaurant's exit, one of the waitresses I'd talked to came over. "You want to hear a joke?"

I didn't, but I nodded politely.

"On the radio," she said. "The local weatherman. He claims it's hot and clear."

I shook my head, confused.

"The storm." She laughed. "He doesn't know it's raining. All his instruments, his radar and his charts, he hasn't brains enough to look outside and see what kind of day it is. If anything, the rain got worse." She laughed again. "The biggest joke—that dummy's my husband."

I laughed to be agreeable and went to the lobby.

It was crowded. More rain-drenched travelers pushed in, cursing the weather. They tugged at dripping clothes and bunched before the motel's counter, wanting rooms.

I squeezed past them, stopping at the big glass door, squinting out at the wildest rain I'd ever seen. Above the exclamations of the crowd, I heard the shriek of the wind.

My hand reached for the door.

It hesitated. I really didn't want to go out.

The skinny desk clerk suddenly stood next to me. "It could be you're not interested," he said.

I frowned, surprised.

"We're renting rooms so fast we'll soon be all full up," he said. "But fair is fair. You got here first. I saved a room. In case you plan on staying."

"I appreciate it. But we're leaving soon."

"You'd better take another look."

I did. Lightning split a tree. The window shook from thunder.

A steaming bath, I thought. A sizzling steak. Warm blankets while my clothes get dry.

"I changed my mind. We'll take that room."

* * *

All night, thunder shook the building. Even with the drapes shut, I saw brilliant streaks of lightning. I slept fitfully, waking with a headache. Six a.m., it was still raining.

On the radio, the weatherman sounded puzzled. As the lightning's static garbled what he said, I learned that Grand Island was suffering the worst storm in its history. Streets were flooded, sewers blocked, basements overflowing. An emergency had been declared, the damage in the millions. But the cause of the storm seemed inexplicable. The weather pattern made no sense. The front was tiny, localized, and stationary. Half a mile outside Grand Island — north and south, east and west — the sky was cloudless.

That last statement was all I needed to know. We quickly dressed and went downstairs to eat. We checked out shortly after seven.

"Driving in this rain?" The desk clerk shook his head. He had the tact not to say, "You're crazy."

"Listen to the radio," I answered. "Half a mile away, the sky is clear."

I'd have stayed if it hadn't been for Gail. Her fear of storms — the constant lightning and thunder — made her frantic.

"Get me out of here."

And so we went.

And almost didn't reach the interstate. The car was hubcap-deep in water. The distributor was damp. I nearly killed the battery before I got the engine started. The brakes were soaked. They failed as I reached the local road. Skidding, blinded, I swerved around the blur of an abandoned truck, missing the entrance to the interstate. Backing up, I barely saw the ditch in time. But finally we headed up the ramp, rising above the flood, doing twenty down the highway.

Jeff was white-faced. I'd bought some comics for him, but he was too scared to read them.

"The odometer," I told him. "Watch the numbers. Half a mile, and we'll be out of this."

I counted tenths of a mile with him. "One, two, three…"

The storm grew darker, stronger. "Four, five, six…"

The numbers felt like broken glass wedged in my throat.

"But Dad, we're half a mile away. The rain's not stopping."

"Just a little farther."

* * *

But instead of ending, it got worse. We had to stop in Lincoln. The next day, the storm persisted. We pressed on to Omaha. We could normally drive from Colorado to our home in Iowa City in two leisurely days.

But *this* trip took us seven long, slow, agonizing days. We had to stop in Omaha and then Des Moines and towns whose names I'd never heard of. When we at last reached home, we felt so exhausted, so frightened, we left our bags in the car and stumbled from the garage to bed.

The rain slashed against the windows. It drummed on the roof. I couldn't sleep. When I peered out, I saw a waterfall from the overflowing eaves. Lightning struck an electricity pole. I settled to my knees and recollected every prayer I'd ever learned and then invented stronger ones.

The electricity was fixed by morning. The phone still worked. Gail called a friend and asked a question. As she listened to the answer, I was startled by the way her face shrank and her eyes receded. Mumbling, "Thanks," she set the phone down.

"It's been dry here," she said. "Then last night at eight, the storm began."

"But that's when we arrived. My God, what's happening?"

"Coincidence." Gail frowned. "The storm front moved in our direction. We kept trying to escape. Instead we only followed it."

The fridge was bare. I told Gail I'd get some food and warned Jeff not to go outside.

"But Dad, I want to see my friends."

"Watch television. Don't go out till the rain stops."

"It won't end."

I froze. "What makes you say that?"

"Not today it won't. The sky's too dark. The rain's too hard."

I nodded, relaxing. "Then call your friends. But don't go out."

When I opened the garage door, I watched the torrent. Eight days since I'd seen the sun. Damp clung on me. Gusts angled toward me.

I drove from the garage and was swallowed.

* * *

Gail looked overjoyed when I came back. "It stopped for forty minutes." She grinned with relief.

"Not where I was."

The nearest supermarket was half a mile away. Despite my umbrella and raincoat, I'd been drenched when I lurched through the hissing automatic door of the supermarket. Fighting to catch my breath, I'd fumbled with the inside-out umbrella and muttered to a clerk about the goddamn endless rain.

The clerk hadn't known what I meant. "But it started just a minute ago."

I shuddered, but not from the water dripping off me.

Gail heard me out and paled. Her joy turned into frightened disbelief. "As soon as you came back, the storm began again."

I flinched as the bottom fell out of my soggy grocery bag. Ignoring the cans and boxes of food on the floor, I hurried to find a weather station on the radio. But the announcer's static-garbled voice sounded as bewildered as his counterparts throughout Nebraska.

His report was the same. The weather pattern made no sense. The front was tiny, localized, and stationary. Half a mile away, the sky was cloudless. In a small circumference, however, Iowa City was enduring its most savage storm on record. Downtown streets were…

I shut off the radio.

Thinking frantically, I told Gail I was going to my office at the university to see if I had mail. But my motive was quite different, and I hoped she wouldn't think of it.

She started to speak as Jeff came into the kitchen, interrupting us, his eyes bleak with cabin fever. "Drive me down to Freddie's, Dad?"

I didn't have the heart to tell him no.

At the school, the parking lot was flecked with rain. There weren't any puddles, though. I live a mile away. I went in the English building and asked a secretary, although I knew what she'd tell me.

"No, Mr. Price. All morning it's been clear. The rain's just beginning."

In my office, I phoned home.

"The rain stopped," Gail said. "You won't believe how beautiful the sky is, bright and sunny."

I stared from my office window toward a storm so black and ugly I barely saw the whitecaps on the angry churning river.

Fear coiled in my guts, then hissed and struck.

* * *

The pattern was always the same. No matter where I went, the storm went with me. When I left, the storm left as well. It got worse. Nine days of it. Then ten. Eleven. Twelve. Our basement flooded, as did all the other basements in the district. Streets eroded. There were mudslides. Shingles blew away. Attics leaked. Retaining walls fell over. Lightning struck the electricity poles so often the food spoiled in our freezer. We lit candles. If our stove hadn't used gas, we couldn't have cooked. As in Grand Island, an emergency was declared, the damage so great it couldn't be calculated.

What hurt the most was seeing the effect on Gail and Jeff. The constant chilly dampness gave them colds. I sneezed and sniffled, too, but didn't care about myself because Gail's spirits sank the more it rained. Her eyes became a dismal gray. She had no energy. She put on sweaters and rubbed her listless, aching arms.

Jeff went to bed much earlier than usual. He slept later. He looked thin. His eyes had dark circles.

And he had nightmares. As lightning cracked, his screams woke us. Again the electricity wasn't working. We used flashlights as we hurried to his room.

"Wake up, Jeff! You're only dreaming!"

"The Indian!" Moaning, he rubbed his frightened eyes. Thunder rumbled, making Gail jerk.

28

"What Indian?" I said.

"He warned you."

"Son, I don't know what—"

"In Colorado." Gail turned sharply, startling me with the hollows the darkness cast on her cheeks. "The weather dancer."

"You mean that witch doctor?"

On our trip, we'd stopped in a dingy desert town for gas and seen a meager group of tourists studying a roadside Indian display. A shack, rickety tables, beads and drums and belts. Skeptical, I'd walked across. A scruffy Indian, who looked to be at least a hundred, dressed in threadbare, faded vestments, had chanted gibberish while he danced around a circle of rocks in the dust.

"What's going on?" I asked a woman aiming a camera.

"He's a medicine man. He's dancing to make it rain and end the drought."

I scuffed the dust and glanced at the burning sky. My head ached from the heat and the long, oppressive drive. I'd seen too many sleazy roadside stands, too many Indians ripping off tourists, selling overpriced, inauthentic artifacts. Imperfect turquoise, shoddy silver. They'd turned their backs on their heritage and prostituted their traditions.

I didn't care how much they hated us for what we'd done to them. What bothered me was that behind their stoical faces they laughed as they duped us.

Whiskey fumes wafted from the ancient Indian as he clumsily danced around the circle, chanting.

"Can he do it?" Jeff asked. "Can he make it rain?"

"It's a gimmick," I said. "Watch these tourists put money in that so-called native bowl he bought at Sears."

The tourists heard me, their rapt faces suddenly suspicious.

29

The old man stopped performing. "Gimmick?" He glared.

"I didn't mean to speak so loud. I'm sorry if I ruined your routine."

"I made that bowl myself."

"Of course you did."

He lurched across, the whiskey fumes stronger. "You don't think my dance can make it rain?"

"I couldn't care less if you fool these tourists, but my son should know the truth."

"You want convincing?"

"I said I was sorry."

"White men always say they're sorry."

Gail came over, glancing furtively around. Embarrassed, she tugged at my sleeve. "The gas tank's full. Let's go."

I backed away.

"You'll see it rain! You'll pray it stops!" the old man shouted.

Jeff looked terrified, and that made me angry. "Shut your mouth! You scared my son!"

"He wonders if I can make it rain? Watch the sky! I dance for you now! When the lightning strikes, remember me!"

We got in the car. "That crazy coot. Don't let him bother you. The sun cooked his brain."

* * *

"All right, he threatened me. So what?" I asked. "Gail, you surely can't believe he sent this storm. By dancing? Think. It isn't possible."

"Then tell me why it's happening."

"A hundred weather experts tried but can't explain it. How can I?"

"The storm's linked to you. It never leaves you."

30

"It's…" I meant to say "coincidence" again, but the word died in my throat. I studied Gail and Jeff, and in the glare of the flashlights, I realized they blamed me. We were adversaries, both of them against me.

"The rain, Dad. Can't you make it stop?"

I cried when he whispered, "Please."

* * *

Department of Meteorology. It consisted of a full professor, one associate, and one assistant. I'd met the full professor at a cocktail party several years ago. We sometimes played tennis together. On occasion, we had lunch. I knew his office hours and braved the storm to go see him.

Again the parking lot was speckled with increasing raindrops when I got there. I ran through raging wind and shook my raincoat in the lobby of his building. I'd phoned ahead. He was waiting.

Forty-five, freckled, almost bald. In damn fine shape, though, as I knew from many tennis games I'd lost.

"The rain's back." He shook his head disgustedly.

"No explanation yet?"

"I'm supposed to be the expert. Your guess would be as good as mine. If this keeps up, I'll take to reading tea leaves."

"Maybe superstition's…" I wanted to say "the answer," but I couldn't force myself.

"What?" He leaned ahead.

I rubbed my aching forehead. "What causes thunderstorms?"

He shrugged. "Two different fronts collide. One's hot and moist. The other's cold and dry. They bang together so hard they explode. The lightning and thunder are the blast. The rain's the fallout."

"But in *this* case?"

"That's the problem. We don't have two different fronts. Even if we did, the storm would move because of vacuums the winds create. But this storm stays right here. It only shifts a half a mile or so and then comes back. It's forcing us to reassess the rules."

"I don't know how to…" But I told him. Everything.

He frowned. "And you believe this?"

"I'm not sure. My wife and son do. Is it possible?"

He put some papers away. He poured two cups of coffee. He did everything but rearrange his bookshelves.

"Is it possible?" I said.

"If you repeat this, I'll deny it."

"How much crazier can—"

"In the sixties, when I was in grad school, I went on a field trip to Mexico. The mountain valleys have such complicated weather patterns they're perfect for a dissertation. One place gets so much rain the villages are flooded. Ten miles away, another valley gets no rain whatsoever. In one valley I studied, something had gone wrong. It normally had lots of rain. For seven years, though, it had been completely dry. The valley next to it, normally dry, was getting all the rain. No explanation. God knows, I worked hard to find one. People were forced to leave their homes and go where the rain was. In this seventh summer, they stopped hoping the weather would behave the way it used to. They wanted to return to their valley, so they sent for special help. A weather dancer. He claimed to be a descendant of the Mayans. He arrived one day and paced the valley, praying to all the compass points. Where they intersected in the valley's middle, he arranged a wheel of stones. He put on vestments. He danced around the wheel. One day later, it was raining, and the weather pattern went back to the way it used to be. I told myself he'd been lucky, that he'd somehow read the signs of nature and danced when he was positive it would rain. But I saw those clouds rush in, and they were strange. They didn't move on until the streams were flowing and the wells were full. Coincidence? Special knowledge? Who can say? But it troubles me when I think about what happened in that valley."

"Then the Indian I met could cause this storm?"

"Who knows? Look, I'm a scientist. I trust in facts. But sometimes superstition's a word we use for science we don't understand."

"What happens if the storm continues, if it doesn't stop?"

"Whoever lives beneath it will have to move, or else they'll die."

"But what if it follows someone?"

"You really believe it would?"

"It does!"

He studied me. "You ever hear of a superstorm?"

Dismayed, I shook my head.

"On rare occasions, several storms will climb on top of each other. They can tower as high as seven miles."

I felt my heart lurch.

"But this storm's already climbed that high. It's heading up to ten miles now. It'll soon tear houses from foundations. It'll level everything. A stationary half-mile-wide tornado."

"If I'm right, though, if the old man wants to punish me, I can't escape. Unless my wife and son are separate from me, they'll die, too."

"Assuming you're right. But I have to emphasize. There's no scientific reason to believe your theory."

"I think I'm crazy."

* * *

Eliminate the probable, then the possible. What's left must be the explanation. Either Gail and Jeff would die, or they'd have to leave me. But I couldn't bear losing them.

I knew what I had to do. I struggled through the storm to get back home. Jeff was feverish. Gail kept coughing, glaring at me in accusation.

They argued when I told them, but in desperation, they agreed.

"If what we think is true," I said, "once I'm gone, the storm'll stop. You'll see the sun again."

"But what about you? What'll happen?"

"Pray for me."

* * *

The interstate again, heading west. The storm, of course, went with me.

Iowa. Nebraska. It took me three insane, disastrous weeks to get to Colorado. Driving through rain-swept mountains was a nightmare. But I finally reached that dingy desert town. I found that sleazy roadside stand.

No trinkets, no beads. As the storm raged, turning dust to mud, I searched the town, begging for information. "That old Indian. The weather dancer."

"He took sick," a store owner said.

"Where is he?"

"How should I know? Try the reservation."

It was fifteen miles away. The road was serpentine, narrow, and mucky. I passed rocks so hot they steamed from rain. The car slid, crashing into a ditch, resting on its driveshaft. I ran through lightning and thunder, drenched and moaning when I stumbled to the largest building on the reservation. It was low and wide, made from stone. I pounded on the door. A man in a uniform opened it, the agent for the government.

I told him.

He frowned with suspicion. Turning, he spoke a different language to some Indians in the office. They answered.

He nodded. "You must want him bad," he said, "if you came out here in this storm. You're almost out of time. The old man's dying."

In the reservation's hospital, the old man lay motionless under sheets, an IV in his arm. Shriveled, he looked like a dry, empty corn husk. He slowly opened his eyes. They gleamed with recognition.

"I believe you now," I said. "Please, make the rain stop."

He breathed in pain.

"My wife and son believe. It isn't fair to make them suffer. Please." My voice rose. "I shouldn't have said what I did. I'm sorry. Make it stop."

The old map squirmed.

I sank to my knees, kissed his hand, and sobbed. "I know I don't deserve it. But I'm begging you. I've learned my lesson. Stop the rain."

The old man studied me and slowly nodded. The doctor tried to restrain him, but the old man's strength was extraordinary. He crawled from bed. He hobbled. Slowly, in evident pain, he chanted and danced.

The lightning and thunder worsened. Rain slashed the windows. The old man strained to dance harder. The frenzy of the storm increased. Its strident fury soared. It reached a climax, hung there—and stopped.

The old man fell. Gasping, I ran to him and helped the doctor lift him into bed.

The doctor scowled. "You almost killed him."

"He isn't dead?"

"No thanks to you."

But that was the word I used: "Thanks." To the old man and the powers in the sky.

I left the hospital. The sun, a once common sight, overwhelmed me.

* * *

Four days later, back in Iowa, I got the call. The agent from the government. He thought I'd want to know. That morning, the old man had died.

I turned to Gail and Jeff. Their colds were gone. From warm sunny weeks while I was away, their skin was brown again. They seemed to have forgotten how the nightmare had nearly destroyed us, more than just our lives, our love. Indeed they were now skeptical about the Indian and told me that the rain would have stopped, no matter what I did.

But they hadn't been in the hospital to see him dance. They didn't understand.

I set the phone down and swallowed with sadness. Stepping from our house — it rests on a hill — I peered in admiration toward the glorious sky.

I turned and faltered.

To the west, a massive cloudbank approached, dark and thick and roiling. Wind began, bringing a chill.

September twelfth. The temperature was seventy-eight. It dropped to fifty, then thirty-two.

The rain had stopped. The old man had done what I asked. But I hadn't counted on his sense of humor.

He had stopped the rain, all right.

But I had a terrible feeling that the snow would never end.

Mr. Mumblety-Peg
Tim Curran

It was a lovely spring afternoon, the May sunshine was golden, the grass was green, and the air was sweet with honeysuckle. Gale Anzalone woke from her refreshing two-hour nap, rubbing sleep from her eyes, and grinning. Genuinely happy, genuinely content, and genuinely optimistic. The kids would be home from school in an hour and she needed to marinate the chicken breasts so they'd be ready to throw on the grill when John came home at five.

It was going to be a good night, a real good night.

The sitter — Mrs. Jacobs from next door — would be over at seven and they would make the theater by eight easily for the new Paul Rudd movie. Scratching her head, still grinning, knowing all was right with the world, Gale went downstairs. It wasn't until she got there that the smile faded from her lips.

She smelled something burnt, something pungent.

An odor like that certainly didn't belong on a golden May afternoon like this. It was nasty, it was hot, it was practically burning. *Sulfurous,* was the word that occurred to her. A thousand fetid rotten eggs fuming in a barrel.

She paused there at the bottom of the steps, unable to go farther.

It's just some weird smell that blew in from outside, reason told her. *Nothing to freak out about.*

But her instinct—which most assuredly had its back up now—didn't agree. Something had changed. Something had shifted. Spring had been pushed aside and a season of darkness and malevolence had inserted itself. Foulness was its perfume.

As absurd as it sounded, she believed this and could not shake that belief. It was more than the smell, but the *feel* of things. What had been soft and silky before was now gritty and coarse.

Steeling herself for she knew not what, she stepped down onto the landing and then took two steps across the polished hardwood floor. The first thing she became aware of was the silence of the neighborhood outside. It seemed to press up against the house. No birds sang in the trees, no bees buzzed in the garden. Mr. Feister was not edging his sidewalks or trimming his shrubs. Christ, there wasn't even the sound of a car in the distance.

It was as if the house was disconnected from the real world, placed under a dusty glass dome.

So when she heard the sound from the living room, it seemed very *loud.* There was no mistaking what it was: the sound of a man humming. Humming in that contented way people do when they're doing something they love that fills them with great joy, a woman paging through a photo album or a man arranging his tackle box.

"Hmmm-hmmm, hmmm-hmmm, hmmm-hmmm…"

There was absolutely no musical rhythm to it. It was perfectly flat, perfectly toneless.

This is ridiculous, Gale told herself. *What's wrong with you?*

She stepped into the living room and the hot, reeking stench of sulfur fumes almost put her to her knees. There was a man leaning up against the mantle looking at photos of the twins—Caden and Cassidy awestruck at Christmas, their fifth birthday blowout at Chuck E. Cheese's—and humming happily. He was tall, almost emaciated, wearing a black sharkskin suit and pointy-toed leather shoes with silver cleats at the tip. His face was perfectly white, perfectly bloodless, and...perfectly awful.

"Good afternoon, fine lady," he said, his voice oiled and smooth. "I was just admiring your nice little home and your fine plump children. *Especially* the children."

He smiled sardonically as he said this, his lips swollen and juicy like peeled snakes, a droplet of drool running from them.

"Cassidy is the girl and Caden is the boy. Nice names. Very modern, very chic, very trendy...no John and Mary for your children, eh? I like that. Keep up with the times and reject the old ways. I dislike biblical names anyway."

Gale's entire body was shaking. Her knees felt like they were filled with water, her ankles made of rubber. The blood had drained from her head and she was woozy. "Get the hell out...get the hell out of my house."

He shook his head. "I'm afraid that's not possible at this juncture. I'll be staying, dear heart, and you'll be sitting."

How it happened, she wasn't sure. It seemed she blinked her eyes and she *was* sitting down. Her ass was plunked on the sofa and she had no memory of putting it there.

"Who are you?" she heard her voice ask.

He considered this, tapping one long white finger to his chin. "Yes...who am I? Why...why I'm Mr. Mumblety-Peg. Isn't that rich? Mr. *Mumblety-Peg!* You're familiar with the boy's game of chance played with a knife? Well, there you are. I've been so many people, Mr. Black and Mr. White, Mr. Fish and Mr. Gacy...but I do like Mr. Mumblety-Peg. Very sing-song, eh? Has a certain fairy-tale quality to it, wouldn't you agree? *Mr. Mumblety-Peg. La-la-la-la.*"

He was insane. He was some fucking nutjob that had escaped from an insane asylum, she decided. The thing to do was to play along with him and humor him, get him out of the house before the kids got home.

"I once watched two boys play mumblety-peg," he went on, touching a skeletal finger to the tip of his nose. "One of them stabbed himself in the leg. When his blood ran, I knew he was the one. I brined him in a plastic bag for three days with a mixture of cold water, Kosher salt, ginger, cinnamon, cloves, and cracked black pepper. Then I slow-roasted him for twelve hours. He was tender, juicy, and absolutely delicious!"

Gale's breath was barely coming by this point. "Please...*please,* don't hurt me. I'll do whatever you say."

"Of course you will, my duck, of course you will." He turned from her, studying the photographs on the mantle again, licking his lips with a pink worming tongue that looked oddly swollen like an engorged leech. He was holding a pair of golden-rimmed pince-nez spectacles up to his eyes. "Very nice," he said, sliding them into his pocket. Then he looked at Gale and the intensity of his eyes made her bowels creep.

"What...what do you want?"

"It's not so much a matter of what I want, my dear, but what *you* want. You see, the road ahead for you is quite dark indeed. I'm sorry to say that your husband will soon lose his job and you'll be forced to relocate to an inner city neighborhood where your daughter will be kidnapped and murdered—"

"Shut up!" she cried. "Just *shut...up!*"

He explained that it didn't have to be that way at all. If she cooperated, a bargain could be struck and John would not lose his job, in fact he would be offered a lucrative regional director's position with a salary of half a million a year and her daughter would not only grow up healthy and safe, but attend medical school and produce three fine golden-haired grandchildren.

"That is, if you cooperate."

He offered her a toothy grin and her stomach rolled over. She saw that his gums were not pink, but red like raw meat and that his teeth were narrow and peglike, not sharp like those of a monster but serrated like a shark's.

"Now to business. As I said, it's not so much a matter of what I want, but what you want. Now there's no need for your dear loving John to lose his job and you to lose your daughter and your mind. In fact, all of this—" he spread his long, almost surgically thin hands about expansively "—can be preserved. If you give me what I want, I'll protect what you love. Simple, no?"

By this point, Gale was certain she had lost her mind. This couldn't be happening. This…this…freak…this *monster*…he just couldn't walk into people's homes and say these awful things. Things like this just didn't happen.

"Ah, but they do happen, dear lady," Mr. Mumblety-Peg assured her, his white face creasing into a grin. "But there's no need for unpleasantries. If you give me what I want, I'll give you what you want. You have two fine plump children. I want one of them."

Gale just sat there, shaking. It felt like something had broken loose in her chest. Her stomach was a solid ball of concrete. Her lips were opening and closing like those of a fish suffocating on a beach. A sobbing sound was coming from her throat.

Mr. Mumblety-Peg offered her the narrow grin of a corpse, one that had starved to death. "You see, I wish to eat one of your children. I do so enjoy fine, juicy chavy. There's nothing quite like it. Rather like Kobe beef from Japan, eh? Well-marbled, tender, and exquisitely juicy." Then, like a magician, he produced a large, well-thumbed book out of thin air. Its hide covers glistened with oily secretions, the pages crumbling as he turned them. "Listen, if you would. *Kid Wellington with Savory Red Wine Sauce.* Mmmm. This requires six thinly sliced kid tenderloin filets seasoned with salt and garlic to lock in their juices. No need to add oil and clog up the arteries, they'll fry fine in their own fat. Now a few shanks of liver, a sliver or two of Peppadew, a pinch of smoked paprika, a splash of blood consommé and…why, my pet, you look positively green."

"Get…out of my house," Gale breathed, her throat feeling sandy and raw. "GET OUT OF MY FUCKING HOUSE!"

He closed his book and with a quick slight of hand, it vanished. "Ah, your motherly protective impulses are offended. Why, we can't have that. You want to run and find help? Do so. Nothing's holding you there. Seek assistance! Get the police and neighbors and torch-wielding peasants! I'll wait…and when you accept your lost cause, then we'll get down to business."

* * *

Gale didn't leap from the sofa; she nearly rocketed.

She flew into the air and banged her knee on an end table, tripped, fell and crawled to the door and right out onto the porch. She found her feet as she went down the steps…into a world of graveyard silence. Nothing moved, nothing stirred. There was not so much as a breeze. Cardinals did not sing in the trees and bees did not buzz amongst the witch hazel and crocuses. No cars, no dogs barking, no movement of any kind.

A nightmare, I'm trapped in a nightmare.

44

But if it indeed was a nightmare, then it was a special kind of three-dimensional nightmare with absolute physical reality. Her mind was tripping over itself, trying to make sense, trying to put this all in some sort of sane perspective and failing miserably. She stopped there on the sidewalk, frantic and powerless and perfectly helpless. She didn't know what to do. *This world isn't alive,* she heard a voice in her head say. *It's been embalmed.* And the very idea of that sent cold chills up her spine and over the backs of her arms. It was ridiculous, of course, but the very idea persisted. Nothing seemed right, nothing felt right. Even the houses up and down the street looked...*off* somehow. Almost like photographs that were slightly out-of-focus. The sun above had changed, too. It was the yellow of an infected sore.

Move!

Yes, that was the thing. She dashed next door to the Jacobs' house. Old Gil would be on the porch in his rocker reading the paper and Jeanne would be in the kitchen, probably making some treat to bring with her tonight while she sat Cassidy and Caden. Gale was certain of this and she wasn't wrong. Gil *was* sitting on his rocker with the paper gripped in his hands...but his head was sitting on the little table next to him, mouth frozen in an agonized grin, one eye swollen shut, the other open with glassy fear. Blood spattered his face like freckles. And as absolutely horrible as that was, what was probably worse was that his headless body rocked back and forth, back and forth in the chair with an eerie cadence.

With a strangled cry, Gale stumbled away across the yard shouting, "IS THERE ANYBODY? ANYBODY AT ALL?" Then she was across the street, sighting Mr. Feister bending over his carefully squared boxwood hedges. She called his name again and again as she ran over to him, but he did not move and the closer she got the more a sense of crawling dread moved through her belly. Wait…he *was* moving. He was clipping away, highly motivated with his yardwork as usual.

"*Oh…Jesus,*" she said when she got close to him.

Like Mr. Rodgers, he had no head, but that didn't stop him from chopping away at his hedges. Without eyes to guide him, he was mutilating them, scissoring ragged wedges free.

It was at this point that Gale screamed.

She backed away, terrified that Mr. Feister would take notice of her and do to her what he was doing to his beloved hedges. *Chop, chop, chop,* he went. Gale stumbled out onto the sidewalk, everything seeming to fly apart in her head and that's when she saw someone coming up the walk. It was Jim Kang from down the block, the neighborhood pervert. Unmarried and unwanted, he leered at every woman in the neighborhood. And it was no secret that he peered from his blinds every day to watch the high school girls passing by. He had once said something to Bart Blazer's leggy sixteen-year-old daughter, Shayla. What that was no one knew. They only knew that Bart had stormed over there and punched Kang in the face and everyone heard him say, "*Next time, I'll cut your balls off.*"

Enough said.

Jim Kang would have been the last person Gale would have sought help from. But here she was running to him, taking hold of him and babbling out the horrors of her day.

* * *

Kang, of course, knew there was something funny in the neighborhood. The silence had tipped him off as it had Gale. But it wasn't until he heard her shouting in the street and then screaming that he realized just how bad things were. She clung to him, yammering on incoherently about a man in her house, an awful man that was threatening her. He held onto her, liking the feel of her body under her T-shirt. He'd always had his eye on her. The blonde hair and blue eyes, that come-hither MILF look about her.

"You've gotta help me! *You've got to!*" she demanded.

He decided that the first thing she needed was a good slap across the face to straighten her shit out. That was the first thing. The second thing they'd discuss when he was inside her house and had scared the big bad man away.

"All right, all right," he said. "Let's go see what this is about."

She continued to cling to him like something to wear — he would be wearing her later, that was for sure — and he walked with her over to her house. She kept going on about dead people and monsters, one breast brushing over his bare arm and exciting him at the possibilities. Christ, she wasn't even wearing a bra. All he'd have to do is pull her shirt up and then — well, there would be time for that, wouldn't there? He'd help her, but nothing came for free as they said.

"You need to relax," he told her, slapping his garden trowel against his leg. "Just take it easy."

But all that did was get her going again about cannibals and headless people, of all things. He didn't know Gale very well. She'd always turned away from him like he was a communicable disease. Maybe she was crazy. Maybe she had some kind of mental illness. If that was the case, it might be useful.

"Inside?" he said when they got to her porch.

She was breathing very hard and it excited him. "Yes…he's in there. He's out of his mind. He's dangerous."

Kang didn't know what to think. The things she was saying made no sense. Yet, *something* was going on. The neighborhood was unnaturally quiet. Even the air felt funny, come to think of it. And there was no getting past the fact that Gale was clearly terrified. Clutching his trowel tightly now, he went up the steps with her right behind him. He entered the house and saw nothing at all. The living room was neat as a pin other than a magazine on the floor and an end table slid three or four inches out of position by the sofa. There was certainly no big bad boogeyman to be found. The only thing that really gave him pause was a mephitic stench that ghosted in the air. It was so strong he took a step back...then it was just gone.

"Okay," he said, looking around. "Where's the intruder?"

Gale stumbled about, shaking her head slightly. Her eyes looked glazed like those of a stunned cow. She kept opening and closing her mouth. "I swear to God he was here. He *was!*"

Kang grinned. "Well, he's gone now." He stared at her breasts under her T-shirt, perspiration beading his upper lip like dew. "Tell you what, let's go look upstairs and make sure he's not in your bedroom. That's how we should start this."

But she just didn't seem to get it. She kept shaking her head from side to side. "He was here," she said. "I know he was here."

Kang grinned, then he saw the look on Gale's face and he heard what sounded like a step on the parquet floor behind him, then another. And in his fevered brain, a voice said, *sounds like dress shoes, a man in dress shoes.* As he thought that, a horrible, fetid stink rose up around him. Hell, it enveloped him—like smoldering fumes of sulfur and melting pig iron. That's what he smelled at first. About the time his brain identified it, it became something like exotic spices stored away in a cupboard then meat looping with worms.

All of this happened in maybe two seconds.

As he tried to turn, he found that he couldn't. He was rooted to the spot, his widening eyes staring at Gale's horrified face which reminded him somehow of the faces of soldiers from the trenches of World War I. Faces bleached from atrocity. It was at that precise moment as his insides went loose with fear that he saw an image form in his mind that was quite clear and quite lucid. He saw a man standing behind him—a tall cadaverous man with a pale, waxen face and the rouged red lips of a puppet. His eyes were huge and glossy black set in suckering red sockets like puckered mouths. In his hand he held a garden trowel that was identical to the one Kang himself held…except that, as Kang's eyes darted down, he saw he held no trowel. The boogeyman had taken it from him. *No, you gave it to him when he asked.* But that was insane because he had never spoken to him or saw him before in his life. Yet…the memory was there. That face—white, smooth, unlined—and the eyes—huge, bulging, glistening with black aqueous fluid—and the mouth—lips pink and juicy like raw mince drawing back from pearly white teeth serrated like steak knives—and the voice—soft, silken, hissing: *"Place the trowel in my hand, there's a good fellow. Set it in my palm."* And he had. Oh, God yes, he *had*. Because as the boogeyman spoke, his words became ice tongs that gripped Kang's heart, applying a firm and deadly pressure.

The memory was as real as it was devastating. And now he could see the boogeyman rising up behind him, a black and narrow shadow that expanded like a balloon filling with helium until it became a distorted figure that held the trowel and brought it down with lethal force.

Kang cried out as whatever spell that held him was broken.

He ducked as the trowel sought his throat and it scratched over his cranium, peeling a strip of scalp and hair free and making him cry out. He went to his knees and it didn't seem to be a conscious decision on his part. He heard Gale scream and then he felt the trowel spear into his neck. The agony of it was white-hot and total. His left arm went to rubber and his equilibrium was gone. His head spun and cold sweat ran down his face. The boogeyman had not struck by chance. There was no chance involved in it whatsoever. It was calculated and directed with absolute precision, the blade punching into his neck where it met his shoulder and slicing through the brachial plexus nerves and rendering his left arm useless.

Long before Kang could even make sense of this, the trowel came down again. He could hear it slice through the air like a swinging pendulum in an old AIP Poe film. This time it pierced the other side of his neck, shearing the brachial plexus nerves that controlled his right arm. Now that arm was rubbery, too. It hung at his side like a limp rubber band. Blood that was brilliant red like fake Halloween vampire blood spilled down the front of his shirt. It felt hot, nearly burning as it followed the line of his spine down to the back of his pants.

Now the boogeyman was in front of him and his smooth white face was ravaged and split open with jagged seams, the skin sloughing off in strips like birch bark. His eyes were not so much black now as purple like clotted blood, his teeth long and silver and dagger-shaped like the tines of roasting forks. There seemed to be dozens and dozens of them and the perfectly nightmarish and disturbing thing was that they were in motion. The sharpened silver prongs were jutting in and out of the gums like the needles of a sewing machine. There was a rhythm to it, ten or twelve teeth in the upper and lower jaw sticking out as others retreated next to them, over and over.

Kang didn't have much time to think about that because suddenly the mouth yawned wide like the maw of a crocodile and those teeth impaled his face, skewering him, piercing deep until they scraped against his skull as they came together. He had about enough time to see his blood spatter against the monster's face before his mind closed-up like a clamshell and he went out cold.

But just before he did, a hysterical voice in his head cried out, *he's eating me, he's goddamn well eating me…*

* * *

How Gale managed to stay on her feet was a mystery. From the moment Kang and she entered the living room until now was probably only two or three minutes and each of them a hallucinogenic blur. She stood there not just in shock but something beyond shock. Her nerves had been replaced with burning electric wires and her guts felt like hot glass. With unblinking eyes that felt painted on, she was staring down at Kang. Despite what Mr. Mumblety-Peg had done to him, he actually managed to crawl four or five feet, leaving a smeared blood trail. Though maybe *crawl* wasn't accurate…*slink* was more like it, a flaccid sort of locomotion.

Then the Mr. Mumblety-Peg thing swallowed Kang's face, chuckled under his breath, and by the time he was done doing that, he looked like he had originally: depraved and corpselike but certainly not monstrous. "Do you realize, my dove, that had I not been here to protect your virtue, he would have raped you?" He dismissed this with a wave of his hand. "No matter. No need to thank me. Good riddance to bad rubbish, as they say. Now, no more games. No more interruptions." He peered at the photos of the twins on the mantle like a snake eyeing a mouse hole. "Let us get to the…ah…*meat* of the matter, shall we?"

Still, Gale stood there. She could not move. She was completely locked down and utterly helpless. She did not know what to do.

Mr. Mumblety-Peg stepped over Kang who was not quite dead yet. Blood still ran from the gored hole where his face had once been. He trembled slightly. Now and again, one of his legs would jerk.

"Enough of that," said Mr. Mumblety-Peg. He pointed one sallow finger at Kang and Kang went very quickly from being a badly-used living thing to a badly-used corpse. The change was quite quick. Kang not only went still but he withered like a bush in a terrible drought. The blood that glistened on him and pooled around him dried to a sticky film and then went brown and flaked away. His flesh shriveled to the bones beneath. His eyes pulled into his skull and his hair fell out like the needles of a dead Christmas tree. It happened very quickly. He fell into himself and a puff of noisome dust rose from his remains.

Mr. Mumblety-Peg arched an eyebrow and said, "So." He turned to Gale once again and put eyes on her like hot black smoke. "Down to business. You have two fine children and I want one of them. Choose, dear lady, choose. If you do not, I shall take both of them and I'll take them in front of you. I'll chew on their raw livers and slake my thirst with their blood. I'll disembowel them and suck the marrow from their bones. The bus will be here in less than fifteen minutes. Which shall it be? I'd prefer the girl. Caden appears a bit stringy. Stringy boys have a decidedly gamey taste, I prefer fat little girls whom stew nicely in their own sweet juices. Choose, dove, choose."

The insane part was that as terrible as the things he said were, what brought her out of it like a slap across

the face was the fact that he called Cassidy *fat*. She was
not fat. Plump, surely, but not fat. Gale had been the
same way as a little girl. When her teenage years rolled
around, she transformed into a tall and leggy young lady
that the boys fell over themselves to get near. And it
would be the same with Cassidy, she knew.

If Cassidy lived to her teenage years.

Mr. Mumblety-Peg awaited an answer, studying the
face of an antique brass pocket watch, humming happily,
anticipating the grand feast to come. And the most
delicious and satisfying part of it was that he was letting
Gale damn herself. In choosing, she would destroy
herself spiritually and the very idea made him feel
already full and fat.

As he waited, something occurred to her in her
manic desperation — this was *her* fight. That's why Kang
had been powerless against the demon. Only she could
fight for her children. And that made her think of faith.
She hadn't been to church since she was a child. Religion
and its trappings had very little place in her world, yet
she always believed that she did have faith. Whether it
was in a higher being or the power of her own spirit, she
was not sure. But it was there and she could feel it now.
But how did you fight this monster? She had no Bibles or
crucifixes. *All I have is myself and what I believe in.* She was
a stay-at-home mom, what had once been called a
housewife and what her own mother referred to as a
domestic engineer. She could hear her mother's voice
right now. *Don't let people fool you, dear. Taking care of a
house and a family is more demanding than any profession in
the world. You have to be all things to all people at all times.
Keeping your house clean and putting good meals on the table
is the least of your worries. You have to stand ready at all times
with a broom in your hands to sweep out whatever bad dirt
tries to blow in through the door.* Yes, yes it was true. Of
course, her mother was being metaphorical when she

referred to dirt. For *dirt* was anything that threatened your home and loved ones and you were the first line of defense against it.

"Well?" said Mr. Mumblety-Peg. "I await your answer, dear heart."

Gale looked at his evil, grinning face and said, "You can't have either. You can't have my children now or ever."

And was it her imagination or did something about him seem to shrink at her defiance? He glared at her. A picture fell off the wall. One of the windows shattered. A grim shadow spread in her direction and she knew death was coming for her. Mr. Mumblety-Peg's eyes were now a bright, bleeding red and his mouth was filled with silver surgical needles.

She saw her broom leaning up against the wall. The very idea of using it against him was ludicrous, but she knew it was not only her symbol of office but her symbol of faith. She went for it and he tried to stop her, his nails raking over her arm and cutting her open. No matter. She had it. He roared with a freight train sound and a blast of hot, searing wind burned the fine hairs at the nape of her neck. He came for her and she swung the broom at him, hitting him again and again.

"BUT I WILL HAVE THEM!" he screeched. "AND YOU WILL DELIVER THEM TO ME WITH YOUR OWN HAND! IT MUST BE BY YOUR HAND!"

She swung the broom yet again, filled with exhilaration, heat, and energy and he snapped it in half quite easily. She had only the sweeping end of it now with about two feet of jagged broomstick jutting forth and it was this she used. As he launched himself at her, she jabbed it right into his chest and he screamed. God yes, he screamed with agony at the impalement, and blood that was black and steaming exploded into the air in an acidic mist. Black goo bubbled from his eyes and his face became a pulsating fleshy mass, a heaving black tumor that split open with a rotten meat smell and he danced away, leaking and fragmenting and shrieking, little more than a hissing, boiling miasma in a shiny dark suit.

Then…nothing.

Gale went down to her knees, gasping at the expulsion of putrid odor that blew from him and then…and then, she opened her eyes and she could hear not only the birds singing and the bees buzzing happily in the flowerbeds but the rumbling of the school bus coming up the street. By then, the stench of Mr. Mumblety-Peg had faded and she could only smell the sweetness of summer budding and blossoming. *And it was all a dream,* a voice said in her head, but looking down at the three bleeding trenches torn in her arm, she knew it was no dream. Panting, confused, she quickly cleaned up the living room, putting things in their place as was her way. The remains of Kang were gone. Nothing was broken. Nothing was damaged. All was as it should be. Dashing into the bathroom, she wrapped her arm in gauze and then, picking up the broken broom, she stood in the doorway waiting for the bus.

The world had gone back to the way it was.

It was as if nothing had ever happened.

The children came running up the walk and Gale waved to the bus driver. Caden looked at the broom she carried and said, "Nice broom, Mom. Dad better get you a new one." Cassidy, the much more vocal and LOUDER of the twins cried out: "WHAT DID YOU DO TODAY, MAMA?"

Gale smiled. "I cleaned out some dirt."

"NASTY DARN DIRT!" Cassidy said.

Then Gale had collected both of them in her arms, connected to them, empowered by their love and the purity of their innocence. Bad dirt would blow through the door again one day and she would stand ready to face it, broom in hand.

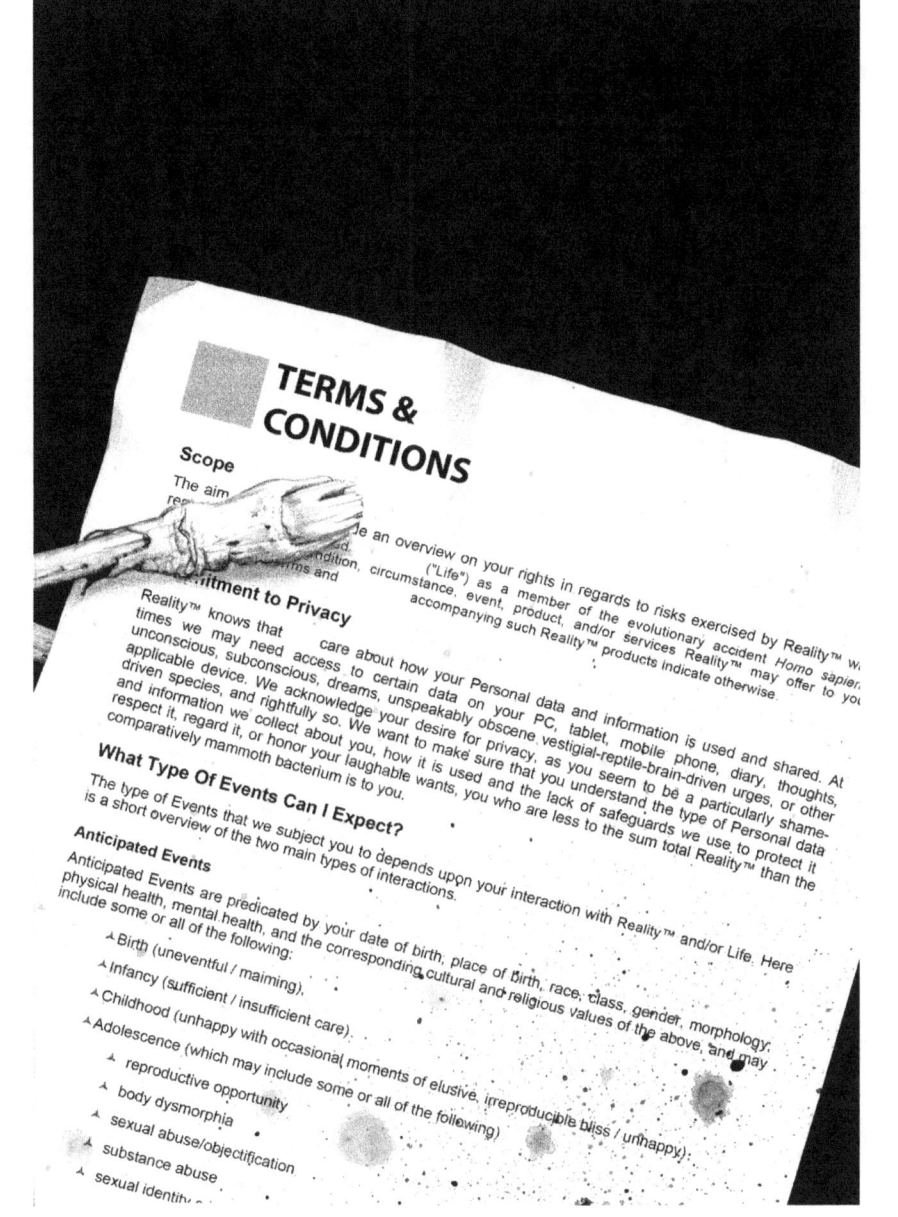

TERMS & CONDITIONS

Scope

The aim ... re... ...de an overview on your rights in regards to risks exercised by Reality™ w... ...dition, circumstance, event, product, and/or services Reality™ may offer to yo... ...ms and ("Life") as a member of the evolutionary accident *Homo sapien*... accompanying such Reality™ products indicate otherwise.

...itment to Privacy

Reality™ knows that ... care about how your Personal data and information is used and shared. At times we may need access to certain data on your PC, tablet, mobile phone, diary, thoughts, unconscious, subconscious, dreams, unspeakably obscene vestigial-reptile-brain-driven urges, or other applicable device. We acknowledge your desire for privacy, as you seem to be a particularly shame-driven species, and rightfully so. We want to make sure that you understand the type of Personal data and information we collect about you, how it is used and the lack of safeguards we use to protect it respect it, regard it, or honor your laughable wants, you who are less to the sum total Reality™ than the comparatively mammoth bacterium is to you.

What Type Of Events Can I Expect?

The type of Events that we subject you to depends upon your interaction with Reality™ and/or Life. Here is a short overview of the two main types of interactions.

Anticipated Events

Anticipated Events are predicated by your date of birth, place of birth, race, class, gender, morphology, physical health, mental health, and the corresponding cultural and religious values of the above, and may include some or all of the following:

⅄ Birth (uneventful / maiming).

⅄ Infancy (sufficient / insufficient care).

⅄ Childhood (unhappy with occasional moments of elusive, irreproducible bliss / unhappy).

⅄ Adolescence (which may include some or all of the following)

  ⅄ reproductive opportunity

  ⅄ body dysmorphia

  ⅄ sexual abuse/objectification

  ⅄ substance abuse

  ⅄ sexual identity ...

Terms And Conditions
Violet LeVoit

Scope

The aim of this is to provide an overview on your rights in regards to risks exercised by Reality™ with respect to your continued existence ("Life") as a member of the evolutionary accident *Homo sapiens* ("Person") and any condition, circumstance, event, product, and/or services Reality™ may offer to you ("Events"), unless terms and conditions accompanying such Reality™ products indicate otherwise.

Commitment to Privacy

Reality™ knows that you care about how your personal data and information is used and shared. At times we may need access to certain data on your PC, tablet, mobile phone, diary, thoughts, unconscious, subconscious, dreams, vestigial-reptile-brain-driven urges, or other applicable device or organ system. We acknowledge your desire for privacy, as you seem to be a particularly shame-driven species, and rightfully so. We want to make sure that you understand the type of personal data and information we collect about you, how it is used and the lack of safeguards we use to protect it, respect it, regard it, or honor your laughable wants, you who are less to the sum total Reality™ than the comparatively mammoth bacterium is to you.

What Type Of Events Can I Expect?

The type of Events that we subject you to depends upon your interaction with Reality™ and/or Life. Here is a short overview of the two main types of interactions.

Anticipated Events

Anticipated Events are predicated by your date of birth, place of birth, race, class, gender, morphology, physical health, mental health, and the corresponding cultural and religious values of the above, and may include some or all of the following:

➢ Birth (uneventful / maiming)
➢ Infancy (sufficient / insufficient care)
➢ Childhood (unhappy with occasional moments of elusive, irreproducible bliss / unhappy)
➢ Adolescence (which may include some or all of the following)
  ➢ reproductive opportunity
  ➢ body dysmorphia
  ➢ sexual abuse/objectification
  ➢ substance abuse
  ➢ sexual identity crisis
  ➢ social ostracization
  ➢ subject to acts of unconscionable cruelty from a peer
  ➢ perpetrating acts of unconscionable cruelty against a peer (from a place of ignorance / with full sadistic awareness)
  ➢ suicide (attempted / successful)

➢ Marriage (tolerable / unhappy)
➢ Work (tolerable / unhappy)
➢ Chronic disease*

Please refer to Table 1-A to determine your eligibility for First World chronic disease (diabetes, obesity, heart disease) or Third World (tuberculosis, Vitamin A deficiency blindness, leaking bowel fistula). Arthritis and AIDS are included in both packages.

Unanticipated Events

Unanticipated Events will compromise most of your Reality™ experience and will include some if not all of the following:

➢ Unexpected Death from:

   ➢ car accident

   ➢ fire

   ➢ falling objects

   ➢ carbon monoxide poisoning

   ➢ alcohol poisoning

   ➢ trampling by marauding elephant

   ➢ crazed lone shooter* or crazed horde of warlords*

   ➢ plane crash

   ➢ your sister's foot slipping too hard on the ignition pedal as she is backing up the car while you stand behind her waggling your fingers and saying "Keep going, keep going"

   ➢ diving into water that seemed clear and blue and limitless from your vantage point on the pier

- ➤ going on an internet dating site and meeting a recent widower who likes Steely Dan and Golden Retrievers and anal rape and asphyxiation

- ➤ eating spinach that was fresh and green and rampant with *E.coli*

- ➤ jumping off a bridge after your tow-headed son ate spinach that was fresh and green and rampant with *E.coli* because you made him eat it but didn't have any yourself because you hate spinach

- ➤ jumping off a bridge because someone doesn't love you

- ➤ jumping off a bridge because someone who once loved you doesn't love you anymore

- ➤ jumping off a bridge because someone who once loved you doesn't love you anymore and also gave you a venereal disease that guarantees no one else will love you again, ever

- ➤ falling off a bridge while you were climbing over the guardrail just because you were just curious to see what people who jump off of bridges see in their last moments

- ➤ asphyxiation because you got confused about whether you could or couldn't eat breakfast the day of your cosmetic surgery that was going to be your new start on life and you choked on regurgitated eggs on the operating table

- ➤ blood clot on plane to honeymoon

- ➤ blood clot on plane to Disneyworld* or refugee camp*

- ➤ blood clot because you saw this thing on Dr. Oz where he said you might not need to take your anticoagulants if you eat kale

- ➢ trampling at rock concert* or food riot*
- ➢ choking on food you like
- ➢ choking on food you don't like and as the blackness swims in front of your eyes you're seized with regret that it wasn't something you actually enjoy
- ➢ an honor-killing because you were caught talking alone with a man who was not a blood relative* (women only)
- ➢ childbirth (women only)
- ➢ being set on fire by a jealous husband who prefers his third concubine over you* (women only)
- ➢ being stabbed to death by your baby's daddy because he doesn't like you dating again (women only)
- ➢ having your throat cut for your refusal to bear male children* (women only)
- ➢ dropping dead from exhaustion after your fifth trip hauling a discarded petrol container full of water from the nearest well back to your village because you're still anemic after your only live birth this year* (women only)
- ➢ being drowned by your older toddler sister because your mother thought you'd be fine in the bathtub together while she took the clothes from the washer and put them in the dryer*
- ➢ passing out in an alley after a binge and being torn apart while still alive but insensate by hyenas* or bath salt addicts*
- ➢ sleep apnea

Unexpected Misery
- ➤ Physical Miseries by:
    - ➤ fire
    - ➤ stroke
    - ➤ tumor
    - ➤ rare skin disease
    - ➤ acid being thrown in your face by a jealous boyfriend
    - ➤ flesh-eating bacteria
    - ➤ genital mutilation incurred by well-meaning, tradition-minded parents
    - ➤ loss of limb incurred in wartime
    - ➤ loss of eye following hunting accident* or coming-of-age ceremony*
    - ➤ ingrown toenail
    - ➤ itchy dry skin in the winter
    - ➤ failing vision
    - ➤ gray hairs that make you look old
    - ➤ facial lines incurred by repeated laughing and frowning and flexing the skin of your face that make you look old
    - ➤ yellowing teeth from a lifetime of drinking coffee and red wine
    - ➤ yellowing teeth and facial lines from a lifetime of pouring another glass of red wine and throwing back your head and laughing heartily "I'd rather enjoy my red wine and hearty laughter than

worry about silly old wrinkles and white teeth"
and quickly downing the puckery merlot before
that feeling of being ugly and old and forgotten
resurfaces.

- ➤ Mental Miseries by:
  - ➤ heartbreak
  - ➤ rejection
  - ➤ dementia
  - ➤ grief
  - ➤ people dying without you telling them you loved
    them, even though you had plenty of chances
  - ➤ liking Becky Alvarado in the third grade and her
    rejection souring you against all other freckled
    girls with shiny, dark curls, thus curdling you
    against three women who were otherwise fated to
    be absolutely perfect girlfriends for you and who
    you could have married instead of sitting alone in
    your apartment at this minute watching *Barely
    Legal Bi Sluts III* and masturbating while full of
    contempt
  - ➤ vague shame over wetting your pants in nursery
    school, kindergarten, first grade, second grade, or
    third grade
  - ➤ not-at-all-vague shame over wetting your pants in
    the fourth grade and beyond
  - ➤ persistent regret about not going on a vision quest
    to meet the ancestors* or grad school*
  - ➤ persistent regret about how the Holocaust* or the
    Rwandan Genocide* proved that when called to

take a moral stand against the face of evil, you are actually a coward

> persistent regret about how the Holocaust* or the Rwandan Genocide* proved that when when called to take a moral stand against the face of evil, you are actually an opportunistic sadist, rapist, and cheerful defecator into the eviscerated chest cavity of still-mewling ethnic minority infants

> persistent lip-quivering terror that even though nothing terrible has happened to you in your life, thank God, knock on wood, you've had a quiet life and things have been good to you, God bless, a good home and a good wife and three beautiful kids and a grandkid on the way and a nice house in Bayonne, not fancy but you're a simple man, that there are terrible things that happen in this world and one day there'll be a knock on the door or not even a knock, they'll just break in, the grinning baby-shitter with blood on his lips, the grandkid gets born with cerebral palsy, your wife will drop dead while cooking dinner and burn a bull's-eye cluster of rings on her cheek from the electric range and you won't even know until you sniff the air and yell "Claudette, is the brisket burning?", you will be having a lovely Sunday afternoon watching the game and suddenly the Jets are losing 9-7 and you get up to take a bathroom break and you piss blood and die of bladder cancer in three months but not before thrashing in a hospital bed for days in a poorly-dialysized hallucination while the catheter burns like a soldering iron and you can feel the cells in your kidneys wither and atrophy, literally feel each one spasm and die, the floor will drop out from this gossamer illusion you call A Good Life,

and Death in all its immutable splendor will come
to take what you were enough of a fool to believe
was rightfully yours

Consult Table 1-A to determine your eligibility.

What Can I Do To Prevent Events?

The execution and duration of events is solely at the
discretion of Reality™. However, it is within your rights
to subscribe to any mental strategy created to overlay a
veneer of comprehension over Events to allow digestion
by your limited, primate mind ("Coping Device")

➢ Religious fervor

➢ Positive affirmations

➢ Psychotic delusion

➢ Illusion of free will

➢ Illusion of divinely proscribed destiny

➢ Other forms of magical thinking

➢ Assuming an affected, adolescent approximation of
   world-weary despair as a hyper-rational armor
   against Reality™ (Note: Void after experiencing
   actual tragedy)

➢ Unaffected existential despair

➢ Railing, weeping, sobbing, rending of garments

➢ Investiture in spouse and/or children as "reason to
   keep on living"

➢ Substance abuse

➢ Yoga and/or Zumba

Acceptance of Terms

By clicking the appropriate box below, I accept that I have read the terms of this agreement. I understand that I did not choose the parameters of Reality™, and in fact have no control over the events that befall me. I also understand if I want to experience love, joy, comfort, pleasure, elation, or satisfaction ("Good Stuff") I must also voluntarily agree to any of the Events aforementioned, and also that none of the Good Stuff is guaranteed. I must also know that, while I may be one of the lucky few who experiences an absolute minimum of Events, I will not escape death or the death of those close to me. It is within my rights for this realization to fill me with inexplicable horror that I am free to ignore or recall as circumstances see fit as I try to navigate a Reality™ that was never meant to accommodate me, that regards my petty hungers and gaping pain with a disregard that could be considered cruel were it not so infinitely impersonal and vacant, and also to know that my hand is pushed, that my cries are futile, that this is the only game in town.

Through means made abundantly clear, I have the right to nullify this agreement at any time.

> Accept   Decline

Hate Me Afire
Thomas Sullivan

The dustrag clouds had been nudging out the sun all afternoon, preventing Logan Tyler from getting his direction. Now a solid gray bank sponged up sunset, threatening to declare night then and there. The beetle-blue needle of his compass made a palsied quarter-circle of East Texas sky before swinging back a full rotation and a half. Nine ninety-five at Sears, leather case included. Haywire.

Nearly two hours had passed since he had begun to search for the road in earnest. There was a grove of oaks near the car, he remembered, and beyond that a peculiar sprinkle of pine hissing garrulously in the wind. But all around him now were denuded hickory trees.

He looked at his companion. The liver-and-white bird dog was too high at the shoulder, too bulky to penetrate dense coverts for long without tiring. They had gone far enough.

"Cold, Robey?"

The dog gave him a cowed look.

"Sun sends its heat ninety-three million miles just to get stopped a thousand feet short," Logan sighed. "Night soon."

They wouldn't starve. He would build a fire to cook the stiffened blue quail stuffed in his game pocket. In the morning he would set out again, following the sun till he reached the road. Nothing to worry about. Another story for long holiday dinners with the nephews and his brother-in-law.

The liver-and-white sniffed each gray stick of kindling gathered and fell to gnawing the shards of bark as fast as Logan stripped them down. When the pile was adequate, Logan improvised tinder out of a pocket calendar and a few handfuls of rusted leaves. They fired easily. In the figurative and literal glow of this small triumph he drew the cold, wooden bird from his pouch and plucked it clean. Then he gutted it with his Buck knife and hurled the trailings into the trees. The dog briefly forayed after, but the woods in the gathering gloom repelled him.

Logan had never seen him balk like that.

Dark, viscous clots drifted overhead. No hint of orange pointed the direction of the vanished sun. A cool breeze crept along the concave floor of the forest bearing a taint of something wet and fungicidal. Man and dog came closer, sharing dinner and what was left in the water bottle. Both knew by this time: neither night nor woods belonged to them. Their ears keyed to the Morse code clack of conspiratorial branches and their eyes returned to the moon-stained limbs of a single, raped tree until it had the moon in its grasp. The dank odor that penetrated the circle of heat settled in their lungs like a killing frost.

Logan slept little. When he awoke the final time it was still dark, though there were gray vaults in the higher reaches of the forest. The fire was a gloomy pulp of ashes.

"What is it?" he managed thickly as the dog growled.

And then the animal was black animation in an ebony corridor of trees.

"Robey!" Logan called in vain.

Far out he thought he saw a flash of red, quickly gone.

"Robey!" he called again, and there was a kind of silence that screamed, a pause in perception that implied an answer.

He didn't know how he knew, but he was absolutely sure something terminal had happened. His dog, his companion. A vibration like the high note of a violin rose in his throat and stuck there. And just like an invitation, the sky suddenly brightened. Logan hurried after through broad shafts of gray light.

Ahead was a dusky permanence with a bit of color in it, not the brief scarlet rent in the air he had glimpsed before but a solid parallelogram of blue. A jackrabbit bounded in successively lower loops to his left, making him wish he had picked up his gun from beside the burned-out fire. But he had thought he would only go a few yards. All at once, the parallelogram emerged through the trees, and he found himself two steps up a hill capped by an ancient cabin with a brightly shingled blue roof.

Upon the mossy perimeter — a little below him actually, because the slope to his right dipped beneath the line of the woods from which he had exited — was an old woman. She was pawing a hole in the earth with a rusted shovel, gurgling to herself. She straightened half a foot at the sight of him, affording him opalescent eyes in eroded flesh on a nut-brown face. There was no greeting whatsoever there, no question, not even surprise. The message was clear and absolute.

Undiluted hate.

He had never seen such hate. Her eyes were two sinkholes in the muddy, furrowed field of her face, writhing and sucking at him. The wrinkles fanned away, splicing across others, twisting serpent trails of which her mouth was only a thin, cruel extension. Her blotched and waxen forehead nested in dense, white eyebrows, and her nose was peculiarly humped like a mound of snow that had begun to melt.

With guillotine quickness, the shovel blade dropped in front of the hole. "Mister," she huffed, "*you* are in Black Day Hollow, and I'm *Nurna*. These are *my* woods. I own them, and I don't allow no trespassers."

"My compass is broken," he said. "I'm lost and I'm looking for my dog."

"Black Day Hollow don't hold for no compass. Burns away directions like it burns away auras." Her eyes opened to reveal yellowed scleras when she spoke the word "auras." "And without *auras*, Nurna can reach you — man, woman or ... dog."

"Must be the mineral deposits," Logan replied dryly and glancing down at the instrument hooked to his belt was surprised to see the needle holding steady.

"Step off the hill," she croaked, the shovel chopping at his feet to dance him down. "*Now* look at your compass! Is that 'mineral deposits'?"

The needle was gyrating again. He returned a step above her. It steadied.

"Black Day Hollow's more than a magnet — *it burns away auras!*" she soared. "Why, you was as naked to me a minute ago as if you was already dead. I could see right into your soul — tinder dry. Wouldn't take much to set it ablaze."

He didn't want to figure that out. Apparently her cabin above them was on a virtual island, a sanctuary from the magnetic irregularity of the neighborhood.

"Robey!" he shouted.

Her face sank into a fresh abyss of simmering hate. "If I give you your dog, will you go?"

His eyes darted up the hill to the cabin.

"Will you go?" she rasped.

"If I get my dog."

"So be it."

The rusted shovel jumped ever so slightly, replanting with a soft "chunk" that hid the hole as before. She rolled her eyes across the green necklace of moss that girded the hill, sidled spryly to a spot and drew an imaginary line with her amber finger.

"He was in the hollow, don't you see. Didn't have no *aura*."

She scooped something up in her right hand, her left paddling him closer.

He saw now that there was a black circle on the ground filled with white dust. Her tightly clenched fist suddenly flung a spume of fine ash in the air.

"There's your dog."

Logan looked at the skinny hand clotted with knuckles and at the chalky stain and into the malevolent stone of her face.

"I don't know what that was from," he said, "but I'm going back to camp to pick up my shotgun, and if Robey isn't there, I'm coming back to look for him."

But he had gone no more than seven steps off the hill when he was gripped with a fever so searing that he sagged and spun around.

What had been merely venomous was now incandescent. Telepathic hate bore into him like an emotional laser. He felt it, smelled it. His own flesh burning. It swelled his tongue, glutted his throat. Shaking his head, his eyes fell on the compass again. It was spinning. *The hill!* He stumbled back up, lost his balance, staggered to a knuckle and a knee. Nurna deflated into a rubbery mask and edged back down into the hollow.

"Get off my hill, fool!"

Spoken out of the miasmatic dawn, her words chilled him. The hill was some kind of sanctuary, but the woods … ? She had halved his universe, reduced it to two dimensions — a circle within a circle. He couldn't leave.

"I'm not helpless," he husked. "And if you've hurt my dog in any way, you'll get the same treatment you gave him."

Nurna's gaping mouth assumed one black shape after another, as if to contain dry laughter.

* * *

He backed away, up the hill. And each time he took a step as if to outflank her and descend back into the hollow, he saw the sinkhole eyes tighten on him. She was totally mad, and this … this *thing* she could do was utterly irrational, but — *dear God, his own flesh burning!* He had felt that, smelled the sickening softening of tissue, sensed the instability of melt and boil inside him. And Robey! If his heart wasn't icy with fear, it would be hot with grief. The white ash. That was Robey?

The sun splayed through the trees behind her when he reached the cabin, throwing two-by-fours of light and shadow that reached their widest point at the base of the hill. *East*, Logan noted from the summit, checking his compass against the sunrise. He looked out to what he thought was the road — a swathe in the trees far to the west. Blue smoke explored the air near that break, and beyond that — almost a part of the ground fog at the horizon — was a slip of white he took to be a lake.

And then he saw that she had come out of the hollow and taken up her digging.

"Hey!" he shouted, hop-stepping down as fast as he could. He had no reason to stop her, except that her furtiveness in sneaking across and now her haste in sloughing away the earth were suspicious.

She raised the shovel against his descent but beat a moderate retreat into the hollow.

He grasped the handles of a bronze urn half out of the ground. "What's this that's so important to you?"

The wrinkles of her face ebbed, but her eyes remained black pearls. "My husband's ashes. Leave it buried."

"You weren't burying it." He tugged a little on the inset top.

"That damn animal of yours was digging it up! I wanted to bury it deeper."

Something clicked dryly in her throat as the urn cover rang loose in his hands. It was as she said, full of ashes.

He whistled. "Must have been a big man."

She simmered in silence.

Resealing the urn, he bore it up the slope to the little shack. If any of this was really happening, if she really had incinerated Robey in some way with her phenomenal hate, then there was no telling what this urn contained. And she wanted it. He wasn't about to give her something she wanted.

* * *

All morning he contemplated the thing. His situation, the urn, Robey, Nurna. He sat outside the cabin with a piece of black bread he had taken from inside, watching her watching him. Clearly she had no power over him in merely mortal terms. Just an old woman living by her wiles. If she challenged him by coming up the hill, it would be a short fight. But one step into that limbo at the bottom where magnetism swirled unfettered, and her energy somehow intensified and took on direction. There she could summon forth both hate and heat, focus it with the sheer power of her venom, and cast it like a molten firebrand from her feral mind.

The shock of what she had done was still hitting him. She had singed his soul, deadened the outposts of his flesh to ashes. He had heard of spontaneous human combustion. Was her obscene talent somehow related to that molecular holocaust?

Moot point. The taste of smoke from his own cremation demo lingered in his nostrils.

Over and over he imagined himself running for his life through the trees toward the western gap where the road and safety lay. He tried to visualize the trunks whose tops were visible to him, imagining how they would look in the dark, mapping their position, memorizing clearings. She would expect him to go for the road, and she would be right. Alternate routes were too long, too complicated. It was going to be a race. He thought of his gun, but last night's camp was hopelessly lost.

It came out the same. The shortest distance between two points. A gauntlet. A gamble. A race in the night.

With deliberate slowness, he walked around to the back of the cabin. There he waited, expecting her to follow around the bottom of the hill, lagging behind because she would have more ground to cover. Thirty seconds passed, a minute. Why wasn't she keeping him in sight? Did she even need to see him in order to set him on fire?

The temptation rose in his breast to make a wild dash for the woods below. If he kept to her blind side, he might have a chance. She couldn't possibly keep up with him if he continued to move around the perimeter of the cabin. He could reverse direction, tire her out until she stopped. But where was she? When he came around to the front again, she was nowhere in sight.

Two can play that game, he thought. If she was hiding among the trees, he could go inside again. Let her wonder what he was up to. But just as he stepped across the threshold, he felt the premonition: *she was already inside waiting for him.* A disturbance in the air, or perhaps a flitting shadow, warned him that the iron skillet he had seen on the potbellied stove was swinging toward his skull. He even threw his hands up at the last second. But the cabin was the same as when he had first gone up the hill.

Yet something had changed.

There was the urn he had sat on the table, the loaf of black bread, and the knife from which he had sliced the end crust. A lone bentwood chair, a gray slate sink and the bed with its filthy green pillow and tattered ticking were just as before, as was the single shelf running the length of the back wall. Feathers and flinty stones lay next to foodstuffs on the shelf that ended in a row of maroon spice tins with faded scrollwork in black. The shell of a turtle emerald green to the point of blackness sat there, as did dozens of dusty and colorless knickknacks, unrecognizable except for a solitary toy — a doll — of bisque and linen the color of old ivory. Three hardwood logs and some sticks of birch were piled on a steamer trunk next to the blackened potbellied stove.

But over all of it, as if Nurna's fetid breath — or perhaps her *aura* — had entered the cabin without her, was a faint yellow haze. Auras. She had repeated that term as if to make it substance. That was what was different now. There was an aura in the cabin.

And he could feel the hate. *Her* hate. Unsettling in the extreme. Immediately he wanted to return to the open air. But, of course, she would know where he was for certain then. And there was just a chance that she hadn't seen him go inside, had been still working her way around the woods following his movements as he circled behind the cabin. He had to keep her guessing as much as she was keeping him in the dark.

The dark.

God help him, if he had to spend the night here. He wouldn't. He just couldn't. He would make his run sometime in the dead of night — not immediately after sundown, but when she had waited for hours, growing weary, her senses distracted by the insects that would by then be eating her alive.

Except that the suggestion of haze in the air was really starting to bother him now, and hour by hour it got worse. By midday it was clearly visible — not midday at all inside the cabin. No longer just turning bright spots into halos, it seemed suddenly to rush together in a thin, obscene vapor. If he stared at the spirals of mist, they lingered and began to assume shapes he didn't want to see — the hint of a face, a serpent lunging in his direction.

No, thank you.

He would close his eyes, and when he opened them again, the twist of ectoplasm would have vanished. But in the aftermath he could taste the vapor, a metallic tang like heated metal. And that made his eyes water.

Thirst came, and visions of a cold well or spring-fed aquifer flowing under the cabin were maddening, but he resolved not to drink out of the tap or from the earthenware jug under the slate tub. Whatever it was that poisoned the land and the air of Black Day Hollow, he wanted as little of it inside him as possible.

* * *

It was perhaps 2 or 3 PM when he started to pace the floor of the cabin. Slowly at first, stopping to peek through the weathered wood near the door, and again through seams in the shrunken and badly chinked boards on the back wall. *Too bad there's no window,* he thought. If only there had been one on the other side of the cabin, Nurna wouldn't know whether he was going to make a break out the front or the back.

80

Too bad there's no window.

And it became a mantra as he circled the table, staying as close to the walls as he could … *no window … too bad there's no window … too bad … no window … too bad … no window.*

The yellow haze made his eyes sting, and there was no water, no water, no water, except the cool crystal aquifer beneath the cabin, and God it was hot in here now — you could almost laugh to think old Nurna needed a potbelly stove in this hellhole — and just then, with the sweat pouring off of Logan Tyler, someone kicked two boards loose in the back wall of the cabin. Kicked them with such fury and violence that they split in half at the crosspiece between studs.

Someone!

Except that he was still alone.

With a sound halfway between a laugh and a sob, he dropped to his haunches and stared at the daylight he had opened up through the split boards.

"Robey, Robey …" he whispered with a shudder.

He sat shaking for a long time, breathing what cool air there was coming through the gap in the wall. And when he rose stiffly again, it was with a little clarity. Even if Nurna had lost track when he went behind the cabin, she must know for certain he was inside — all that thundering around he was doing — and she would have heard him kick the boards in half and circled behind once more to see exactly what he had done. She would know his state of mind and what he intended to do. So now she would have to guess where he would make his break. A 50-50 chance.

For both of them.

* * *

When darkness came, it stole into the cabin like a cataract. The yellow haze dulled and dulled until it had

81

the opaqueness of a murky ocean. He was drowning in it. Dying of thirst and drowning. A fragment of Coleridge's "Rime of the Ancient Mariner" popped into his head: "Water, water, everywhere, And all the boards did shrink; Water, water everywhere, Nor any drop to drink."

But why the smell — that burning-metal smell?

His blurred vision careened around the cabin in the sickening oppressiveness of the yellow haze, assaulting his nose, his taste buds. The metallic tang glutted him. The iron stove was cold, but somewhere metal was burning. And there upon the table sat the urn. The bronze urn. It almost seemed to glow in the dimness. Nurna's husband's ashes were inside.

Only … what if they weren't ashes?

What if they were embers? Given the possibility that the old crone had murdered her spouse in a fit of lethal pique, it took only a slight elaboration on the supernatural to believe that the residue could still be hot with hate. Her hate. Or maybe — and this appealed to Logan — her *husband's* hate!

That fit much better. Whatever passions were at war in this godforsaken magnetic woods and the sanctuary of its knoll, the remains in the urn were not at rest. Inside, something unburied was seething with rage. That was what he had interrupted. She had killed him — her husband — before she killed Robey, and she had been burying him far down the hill when Logan came on the scene because … because something about him wasn't quite dead. Like her venomous hate, her spouse's passion — his *aura* — was potentiated somehow, intensified while still above ground and trying to get out.

He regarded the yellow haze. It WAS getting out!

It was in the cabin, in Logan's lungs, all over him! But it wasn't him that it wanted. It was searching for her.

Logan grabbed a rag of a towel on the edge of the
slate sink and a scorched oven mitt with the thumb
burned off lying on the stove, and carrying them like
pincers to the urn, he clamped onto the thing. Lips
moving in an incoherent prayer, he held it, thinking —
hoping — that it would not lash out in a blind,
murderous fury to incinerate his flesh.

In fact, there was no sensation at all. The rag towel
slipped from his left hand, and then the blackened oven
mitt from his right. His sweating fingers stroked the urn.
It was cold.

Trembling, he turned the lid. Lifted it. What light
was left swimming in the room would not enter the
shadowy opening, but he tipped the urn and brought his
face down far enough to see the moving gray surface that
must have been the ashes he had seen at the base of the
hill. So the yellow haze was not coming from the urn.

And that made him certain now. It was Nurna
herself. She was the yellow haze, and she was collecting
here in the cabin, and she would get him when she was
powerful enough. Just a matter of time. She would
suffocate him, dry him out until he reached the ignition
point for a human being, flesh bursting into flames.

He had to make the run now.

Darkness was full outside but there would be a
moon. She would be able to see. His only advantage
was in choosing whether to charge through the front
door or squeeze through the broken boards at the back of
the cabin and descend the hill. But if she was causing the
yellow haze, she must have been expecting it to drive
him out any moment now. So he must resist a little
longer. Must wait as long as possible.

The long night dragged through the cabin like a
funeral procession. Each time his pulse jumped he
imagined he could feel his blood beginning to boil. Was
the hair on the back of his hand starting to singe or was it

a tiny no-see-um hovering in the dark? It was hot, but he kept his parka on just to shut out the obscene yellow haze, and each trickle of sweat convinced him that his skin was beginning to melt.

Logan Tyler sagged to the floor and crawled to the open space at the back of a ramshackle cabin in a place called Black Day Hollow and sucked in as much of the dank night air from outside as he could. Thicker and thicker grew the yellow haze, stifling even his movements as the smell and tang of burning metal went from cloying in his nostrils to molten in his lungs.

And the last sensation festered in his mind. Why the burning metal? It was not the urn and not the stove. What else was there? Staggering to his feet, he felt up the wall to the shelf.

The first thing his fingers groped over was the smooth face of the doll. He felt its empty smile before moving on to the feathers and the crusty emerald shell of the turtle, and finally — for just an instant before he yanked away — his finger touched the first spice tin. One instant only ... because it burned him.

The smell was intense now — burning metal. The tins. The maroon spice tins with the black scrollwork. Truth pulsed into his fading consciousness. The tins were not for spice. They were for more ashes. Nurna's *other* victims. Forget about a murdered husband. For all Logan knew, they were horribly compatible and Nurna really had been burying his ashes in a moment of whatever passed for grief in the inferno of her charred soul. But not so these ashes in the spice tins with the black scrollwork. No compatibility here. These were innocents.

And they hated her!

Using the rag and the mitt, he dumped the urn on the table and one by one refilled it to the brim with a portion of the ashes from each of the maroon tins. Then he kicked open the door and stood just outside in the refreshing night and bellowed the name of Black Day Hollow's feral queen, like a wolf calling out the moon.

She appeared almost instantly in the moonlight, a white-haired hag of a woman whose face was blacker than the night.

"I want to trade!" he shouted. "Safe passage for your husband's ashes!" He kept his eye on her as he started down, but she retreated into the woods.

The fact that she hadn't answered was telling. She wouldn't do it. Wouldn't trade. But it was too late to stop now, and he wouldn't have trusted her word anyway. Only, he wished he could see her. Once, he thought a tiny point scintillated the air, and he imagined some blind and fragile insect hated out of existence in a disproportionate burst of hell.

Down, down he plummeted on the soft velvet hill, repeating "Nurna" in a steady mantra as if to freeze a half-socialized animal in place. At the bottom, he paused, listening. Katydids. Keening like singing telephone wires on a torrid day. And the wind effervescing through treetops. Silently he circled west over yielding moss until a salt cedar he had noted earlier reared up before him. Adrenalin touched his heart. This was it. The plunge through the woods. A wild, primal alertness pumped through his veins as he lurched into the night.

The moon lay in puddles and he picked out a path with the ease of something nocturnal. The road he had seen from the cabin could not be more than a mile away, he told himself. Invisible branches shrieked over his parka, tinning against the urn, and his heart hammered: "run ... run ... run!"

She picked the spot.

It was a treeless depression drenched in lunar light tangled in tendrils that snaked along the ground. He arrived huffing and puffing, clanging through the brush with the urn held in front of his face. She arose in his path, mute and shrouded.

He nearly fell over himself.

"All I want is to get back to the road," he blubbered.

Her laugh blistered hotly over him as her eyes began pooling light from nowhere. Instantly the parka was uncomfortably warm. The air went vapid in his lungs. He felt himself drying out.

"You bitch ..." he spluttered, beginning to weep. "I'm going to dump your urn. I'm going to throw your husband's ashes all over —"

For just a second, the stream of energy pouring into his body eddied as if encountering a rock. She had stiffened. He staggered up and took two steps. The urn with the transferred ashes of her victims was almost too hot to hold now.

"Give it to me!" she cried.

"Let me go then. You let me be ... and you can have it back. Okay?"

She wasn't going to let him live, he knew as she glided forward. What could a promise mean to such a creature? What could what he was about to do mean for his own soul? And willing his heart cold, he jerked the contents of the urn into her face.

He should have run then. But he didn't. He watched. Because she was gasping and recoiling now. The ashes powdered her hair, her brows, making her contorted face a phantom thing.

"What did ..." she tremoloed. "What —"

But that was as far as she got. There was a puff and an unfurling sound, like a sheet spanking in the breeze. As Logan turned to run, he saw the orange reflection of that sheet flowing against the dark trunks of the hickories and cedars of Black Day Hollow. He tried not to think, to let there be just the path, the woods, the road ahead, and the primal chant that pulsed out of his breast: "run … run … run!"

The Mouth
Ray Garton

"I don't want you to die, Mommy."

The words were spoken so softly — barely more than a whisper — that Emma wasn't sure she'd heard what she thought she'd heard as she shoved wet towels into the dryer. The rumbling of the old washing machine that had come with their new house filled the garage and cast even more doubt on what she'd heard. It had sounded like her daughter, but at the age of about eight or nine. Jodie had stopped calling her "Mommy" when she turned 10. Emma turned to find her standing in the open door, the sunny kitchen behind her, but in spite of the vulnerable, childlike whisper she'd heard, her daughter was fourteen. Not a little girl anymore.

"What did you say, honey?"

A faint register of surprise passed over her round face. "I ... I didn't say — "

"What makes you think I'm in danger of dying, Emma?"

Her mouth opened, then closed.

"What's wrong, honey? Come here."

She came down the three concrete steps to the garage floor and walked around the front of both cars. It was Sunday, so Pete was home and the garage was less spacious than most days of the week.

Jodie's auburn hair fell in waves past her shoulders and Emma stroked it with her right hand. The outer ends of Jodie's eyebrows turned downward. She looked like she might start crying soon.

"You look so sad," Emma said as she put her arms around Jodie and gave her a hug. "What's the matter?"

Her shoulders gave a halfhearted shrug.

"Just having one of those downer days?"

She nodded against Emma's shoulder.

"I hate those. Why don't you go outside? It's a beautiful fall day."

Jodie pulled away and said, "I'm going outside now. I'm ... meeting friends."

"Good. I'm glad you're making friends. Well ... come back in time for dinner, all right?"

She nodded as she left the garage.

Emma finished loading the dryer, then turned it on. By the time she went back inside, Jodie was gone. Phil was watching a game on TV and Donnie was in his room.

She said, "Have you noticed that Jodie seems ... I don't know, depressed lately?"

Without taking his eyes off the screen, he said, "Does she? Well, you've got to remember, she's a teenager. We just moved, which is a big disruption, and don't forget, Jodie did not want to come here. And then there are the books she reads and the movies she watches. Vampires, demons, werewolves. I'd be kind of surprised if she didn't seem a little depressed."

"I guess so. I hope that's all it is."

"Don't worry. She'll be fine."

Emma worried, anyway, as Pete leaned forward in his chair and shouted at the football game.

* * *

Everything about the day was crisp: the air, the leaves, the sound of the neighbor boy's Big Wheels tricycle crunching along the sidewalk, the basketball being bounced by children gathered around a hoop across the street. Jodie walked down the driveway, one hand in the pocket of her turquoise flannel hoodie and the other holding her dog's leash, and turned right at the sidewalk.

Bucky behaved as if everything in sight was new and unfamiliar, something he did every time he left the house. He hurried ahead of her and darted back and forth across the sidewalk as they made their way toward the park. He sniffed a fence post, barked at a frightened-looking tuxedo cat across the street, stopped to pee on the post of a stop sign, sniffed another fence, and barked at another cat. He was a flurry of activity in front of and around Jodie as she walked.

She had been happy about moving into a house that was just down the street from a park. Jodie liked to take long walks alone and that seemed a perfect place for it. She had intended to visit the park once they were unpacked and settled, but her first visit took place sooner than that —in the middle of the second night in her new bed and against her will.

She had been startled awake by a voice that night. She sat up in bed and found that her room was silent. After listening for a moment, it was clear that the entire house was still and her parents and little brother were in bed. Curling up on her right side beneath the covers again, she closed her eyes.

Come here to me.

Jodie bolted upright in her bed, groped for the bedside lamp, and turned it on. It wasn't a large room and there were still some unpacked boxes stacked against the wall. She was alone.

Come here to me now.

Jodie became an explosion of flailing limbs under the covers. She rolled out of bed, hit the floor hard on her back, then crawled on hands and knees toward the closed door. Grabbing the knob with her left hand, she got to her feet, switched on the overhead light, then slowly, fearfully turned around.

The voice had not been loud. It was quiet, intimate. And close. Right next to her. As if someone had been spooning her from behind and had spoken into her ear. The words had been uttered so softly that the voice had no gender. It sounded, in fact, like Jodie herself when she whispered.

She thought, Is this what it's like to go insane? To lose your mind?

She stood there for what felt like a long time, her back pressed against the closed door.

Come to me now or I will kill your dog.

Bucky filled her mind – the small, hyper, floppy-eared mutt she had found as an abandoned puppy behind a gas station when she was nine. She'd named him Buckminster after a man she'd recently seen in a documentary about dolphins, but then decided he might find that a bit embarrassing as a puppy and shortened it to Bucky. She loved Bucky so much that, as she stood in her bedroom staring blankly at her empty bed, she could smell his scent, the way he smelled after being bathed, the terrible breath he had most of the time but especially right after he ate and —

Jodie's body stiffened with such a jolt that her head cracked against the door behind her when she suddenly understood that these were her thoughts, in her voice, but they were being manipulated by someone else.

"Someone who's not me," she whispered, just to see if she could still talk after someone's invisible hands had been groping around in her brain.

Come to me now or I will kill your mother and father.

She imagined a mouth saying those words in her voice, the lips moving around the consonants and vowels, but it was not her mouth. It was a mouth that had grown in the tissue of her brain, the lips taking shape as if sculpted, the gentle dip of the philtrum appearing just above the upper lip — a mouth that had grown in her brain like a tumor. A talking tumor.

Stop thinking so much and come to me. Or there will be some dying.

Jodie quickly dressed in jeans, a sweatshirt, and old running shoes, grabbed a flashlight, and left the house as quietly as she could, only to stand on the front porch and wonder where the hell she was going.

A sense of dread grew outward from her center like a feverish chill and she moved uncertainly down the walk to the driveway. The horrible feeling dissipated as she followed the driveway to the sidewalk, where she stared at the street for a moment before turning her head to the right, then to the left. She turned left down the sidewalk and leaves crackled beneath her feet. After a few steps, that bad feeling returned, a gut-deep sense of sickening apprehension. She stopped, turned slowly, and headed in the other direction. The dread faded. In that way, she was quietly steered through the night to the park.

Jodie crossed the parking lot, where the glow of the tall lights fell on empty slots, and walked by the sign in front that read BURDEN HILL PUBLIC PARK. Into the park, across the flat, green lawn, beneath skeletal trees. Two sides of the park bordered on a dense patch of woods that was fenced off. She crossed the bike path, stopped at the seven-foot-tall chain link fence, and wondered what to do next. Was she expected to climb over it?

She turned right, walked several steps along the fence, and felt the embrace of that dark, frightening dread. She turned around, walked in the opposite direction, and it faded away again. She kept going, shining the flashlight on the fence as she passed, until she found a spot where the chain link had been cut and a bottom corner curled outward slightly. She hunkered down and pushed through to the other side, then got to her feet and headed into the woods.

The flashlight's beam cut through a blackness so thick that it felt membranous. She was steered along a zigzagging route through trees and around clumps of vines. She was not sure how far she walked, but it was farther than she had planned to go and she was beginning to worry about finding her way back when...

She came to an abrupt stop, as if her feet suddenly were frozen to the ground. The light fell on one gray boulder embedded in the earth, then found another about eight feet to the right of the first. Between them, a crack had begun to open in the ground. It began a few inches in front of Jodie's toes and extended for at least six feet between the two rocks, opening in the middle to a width of ten inches or so. In that open center was nothing but darkness and, on each side, gray, dirt-crusted rocks in the earth that resembled a glimpse of neglected teeth behind parted lips.

The sound of gentle movement surrounded Jodie and her chest filled with panic as she swept the light from side to side. Dark figures seeped out of the black night all around her and approached. They were other teenagers and a couple of preadolescents, nine altogether. They formed a semicircle around her.

"We're your neighbors," one of the boys said softly. He was tall and slender, the tallest in the group, and had shaggy black hair that fell to his shoulders.

Jodie's mouth was suddenly dry as she opened it to speak, but she did not know what to say.

"We were all called here, too," he went on. "Just like you. Just like this, in the middle of the night. Each of us." He pointed a finger at the crack in the ground between the rocks. "It's opening again. Should be ready in a week, maybe a little longer. It'll be your turn next."

"My ... my turn for ... what?"

He explained what she would be expected to do. When he was done, they stared at her in the dark, waiting for a response.

Horrified, Jodie shook her head and said, "I can't do that. I ... I can't."

"You have to."

She felt small and naked and afraid. "What happens if I don't?"

The others exchanged meaningful looks before turning to her again.

"A new kid moved to the neighborhood about a year ago," the boy said. "Todd Jarrett. That's what he said. That he just couldn't do it. So he didn't. A week later, his house fell into a sinkhole. Todd and his brother were at school and his mom was at work. But his dad and grandma were home. They were both killed. Their bodies were never found."

Come to me now or I will kill your mother and father.

"That was a year ago. Since then ... well, we do what it tells us now."

That had been ten days ago. Now, hands trembling, Bucky led Jodie into the park on a bright, chilly Sunday afternoon beneath a blue sky being navigated by a fleet of bulging white clouds.

It was time.

* * *

Rolly Pope steered his bike off the street and onto the bike path that wound around the park. He had spent most of the day taking care of the baby while Ashley, miserable with a bad cold, tried to sleep. She'd gotten up that afternoon, still dragging her feet, complaining that she could not sleep because she couldn't breathe through her nose. Sipping a cup of tea, she'd insisted that he get out of the house and get some exercise. He promised not to be gone long. He'd ridden from the house to the park and planned to take a couple of spins around the bike path.

Fall was his favorite time of year, the season that made sitting in an office all day even more frustrating than usual. He preferred to be outdoors, no matter the weather, which made his decision to go into advertising a bit baffling. His father, founder of a successful boutique advertising agency in the city, had pushed hard for it and Rolly had thought it was as good a plan as any. Now he worked at his father's agency and someday would inherit it, but he spent all of his time wanting to be outdoors, riding his bike or jogging or walking or working in the yard — the activity wasn't as important as being outside the walls of whatever building he happened to be in at the moment.

"There's nothing wrong with getting some fresh air and exercise," Dad had told him recently. "But you've got your little girl's future to build now, Roland, so it's time to get serious."

He smiled as the biting air washed over his face. About Jaclyn Marie Pope and her future, Rolly was extremely serious, although the slightest thought of his baby girl spread a giddy smile across his face because it made him think of everything that was to come. First words, first steps, first day of school — nothing but firsts for a while. He wanted to be present for each and every one of them.

To his left, a great expanse of green grass stretched out beneath oak and eucalyptus trees, spotted with clusters of picnic tables and a few concrete barbecue pits. To his right, on the other side of a narrow strip of grass, the tall cyclone fence that ran along the edge of the woods passed by in a blur. The laughter of children fluttered through the park like kaleidoscopes of butterflies, backed up by the strumming of a guitar that faded in and out like a distant AM radio station.

The scream that came from the woods beyond the fence startled him so much that he lost control of his bike for a moment and wobbled along the sidewalk to a clumsy stop. Leaning on his right leg, he turned toward the woods and squinted to see through the chain link.

A turquoise-colored shape hurried out of the shaded woods into the sunlight and rattled the fence by running into it. A teenage girl curled the fingers of both hands through the chain link and looked at him with frightened, glistening eyes.

Sobbing, she said, "Can you help me? Please?"

Rolly got off the bike and walked it over to the fence. "What's wrong?"

"My dog. He's hurt. I can't reach him, I need help. Please, mister, I can't do it by myself. Please."

"But I-I don't know how to get over there."

She bent down and pulled a corner of the chain link aside to make an opening for him. "Through here," she said. She stood and pointed behind her. "He's right in there. It won't take long if you'll help me."

The girl's cheeks were wet with tears and her lips trembled as she looked at him imploringly through the fence. It occurred to Rolly that his baby girl would one day be a teenager, and she probably would have a beloved dog or cat.

"All right," he said, nodding as he leaned the bike against the fence, vaguely worried about leaving it unattended. "Step back so I can come through."

She held the chain link aside and he crawled through on hands and knees, then rose to his feet and brushed his gritty hands together.

"This way," she said, and her slender frame shook with more sobs as she ran into the woods.

Rolly ran after her as she darted left around a cluster of trees, then right around a thick stand of bushes, along the length of a fallen tree. He was about to ask her how much farther when she slowed to a stop.

He reached her side and stared for a moment before saying, "What is that?"

"That's where Bucky is," she said. "He fell in there."

Rolly approached the opening slowly. It seemed inaccurate to call it a hole. It looked more like a rip in the earth, a gash that had been pulled apart and stretched to its limit. It was about ten feet long, maybe a little more, and opened to a width of about the same in the middle. Rocks and roots stuck out of the sheer walls of dirt that descended on each side. He stood at the end of the opening and looked down into cool blackness.

"Your dog fell in there?" he said weakly. He saw little hope if the animal had fallen into the yawning chasm. It seemed to have no bottom.

"Yes, he's at this end and he's just over the edge, here," she said, pointing. She got down on her knees at the end of the chasm and beckoned for him to join her. "Please, you're taller, your arms are longer."

Rolly knelt on her left side, pressed both hands flat on the ground, and peered over the edge. All he saw were more rocks and roots, more dirt dropping straight into darkness.

"I don't see him," he said, turning to her. "Are you sure — "

She was gone.

He heard her sobbing behind him an instant before the sole of her foot slammed flat against his ass and pushed. Rolly was so surprised to be falling that he didn't make a sound before the earth slammed shut around him.

* * *

Peter and Roxanne were in charge of getting rid of the bike, and it was gone before its owner had disappeared into the woods with Jodie. The others gathered around the mouth after it had closed. Now it was nothing more than a shallow furrow in the ground.

"Your family's safe," the tall boy said. His name was Gary.

"For how long?" Jodie said.

"Until it's your turn again."

She wondered when that would be, but she did not ask.

* * *

They were well into a meal of chicken and dumplings and Donnie was telling them about a squirrel he'd seen that day when Emma heard the front door open. Donnie was seven with a fondness for telling stories, and he did not like to be interrupted. As he continued, Emma turned to the doorway and waited.

Jodie's head appeared and she looked into the dining room.

"I told you to be back in time for dinner," Emma said, interrupting Donnie.

Standing in the doorway, Jodie opened her mouth, closed it, opened it again, said, "I'm sorry," then turned and hurried away.

Jodie put her napkin on the table, stood, and went after her. She caught up with her down the hall, in Jodie's bedroom.

"Please tell me what's wrong, Jodie," she said.

Removing her hoodie, Jodie shook her head and said, "It's nothing, I'm fine. Just ... missing my friends, and stuff. You know?"

"I know." Emma went to her and put a hand on her back. She saw that Jodie's eyes were puffy, red, and wet. "You've been crying. Look, honey, are you sure everything's — "

She nodded rapidly. "Yes, yes, everything's fine, Mom. Really. I'm just ... I want you to know ... I love you and dad and I appreciate everything you do and-and-and ... I'm glad you're going to be okay." She threw her arms around Emma and hugged her tightly.

Emma slowly wrapped her arms around Jodie and gave her a squeeze. "You're ... sure everything's okay?"

Jodie pulled back and smiled. "Yes. Now let's eat. I'm hungry."

They went into the dining room and Jodie took her place at the table beside Donnie. She filled her plate as Donnie wrapped up his story.

"Where did you spend the afternoon, Jodie?" Emma said.

"In the park. With some friends."

Emma sighed with satisfaction. "We live near a park, we've got the biggest back yard we've ever had, and now you have new friends. And you didn't want to come, Jodie. I think we'll be very happy here. As long as we decide to be." She looked across at Jodie and added, "Right, honey?"

Looking down at her plate, Jodie lifted her head slowly. The corners of her mouth turned up in a smile, but it was a mechanical gesture with nothing behind it. The smile was not reflected in her eyes as she said, "Yes. I'm sure we'll be happy."

In Hell, An Eye
Gemma Files

In Hell, there is an eye which sees everything — Heaven,
too. Because both "places" lie strictly outside the linear, liminal
considerations of human existence, things tend to overlap.
Possibility piled on probability piled on potentiality, the
poisonous inward curl of a gathering thunderhead's funnel.

In Heaven and Hell, everything happens at once — all
pasts, all presents, all futures. Everything which has, or will,
or is, or might be, or might have been. Everything and
anything, in one endless, timeless moment. Certain events
seem to echo each other, usually inadvertently, though not
always. Patterns emerge like recurring dreams: The same thing
or similar things, in different places, with different people. The
same thing happening twice, three times, a thousand. Now and
then. Then...and now.

Over here, for example —

* * *

—it's 1994, and my latest Summoner lies face-down
and naked within a protective circle on the cold
linoleum-tiled floor of his dead girlfriend's basement
apartment, outflung arms, legs and head marking all five
points of a reversed pentagram. The circle, like the
cursive stream of prayer which rims it, has been lightly
traced in some crusted brown substance; like rust, only

thicker. And stickier. Above, one softly shaded bulb stares down, unblinking.

"Arralu-Allatu, Namtaru, Maskim. Asakku, Utukku, Lammyatu, Maskim. Ekimmu, Gallu-Alu, Maskim."

Four hours past the point of clinical death, and the body on the bed behind him has just reached a state of preliminary rigor mortis. Her skin, pale even in life, is now livid, sheer enough to show her extremities bluing, great purple patches embroidering themselves along the undersides of her back and legs as the blood sinks and pools. Her nails and lips are exactly the same color now, for the first time since they both graduated high school.

White, waxen feet with callused heels and purple-varnished toes poke from the hem of her black velvet nightgown. The Summoner can remember applying that very same shade of polish to those very same toes a month ago; the both of them spider-legged together in a bathtub built for one, hot water sloshing everywhere, Nick Cave moaning low in the background. The same question over and over, set to a repetitive lick of cabaret piano, a drone of bass and bells:

Do...you...love me?
(D'you love me?)
Do...you...LOVE me...
(...like I love you?)

Well, maybe not then. Maybe never. And maybe it doesn't matter a whole fuck of a lot, either, especially now.

Pungent scent of burning lavender candles clumsily overlaid atop a rank nasal spectrum showcasing all three distinct smells of magic—before, during, after. All of which makes it hard to think, let alone breathe, or chant, or concentrate. Yet still he manages, somehow.

(Discipline.)

It's magic, not rocket science. A song anybody can join in with, so long as they're reasonably sure they know the right words.

"Maskim. Maskim. Maskim."

The evocation the Summoner continually chants, learned phonetically and by rote, makes his throat hurt and his forehead burn against the apartment floor's bruisy purple tiles: a harsh, sonorous string of vowels like wind through a nautilus' chambers, wormy cavities spiralling outward without end. The rust-stuff on the pentacle's outermost ring, meanwhile, is (of course) blood—most central of all magical ingredients, most all-purpose of symbolic substances. Because he began this ritual under less-than-perfect circumstances, however, he soon found he couldn't remember whether or not this particular prayer was supposed to work more effectively when written in his own blood, or someone else's...

Desperate times, though; desperate measures. He's always thought well under pressure. So a compromise was reached, back when what little was left in the body on the bed's veins remained uncongealed. A half-full café au lait bowl, dark-stained paring knife, and that tourniquet knot throbbing inside his elbow tell the rest of the story.

Maybe he'll strain too hard on the next verse, he thinks, pop a seam and bleed out, right here and now. Never have to get to the end of this ritual, to see what happens, or doesn't. Never have to find out if the choices he's made were right or wrong, good, bad or indifferent...

Maybe. If he's lucky.

Because: *I found it, baby,* that shed shell behind him told him—over the phone, her voice a bare, hushed murmur—just earlier tonight, maybe five-and-a-half hours previous, six hours tops. *The book. It was in pieces, like they'd cut it up and hidden it...one book hidden inside of fifty other books. That's if you can even call two damn* lists *a book...*

Breathing hard into the receiver, her words fast and almost — yes, *broken* – with amazement, with pleasure at this fresh proof of her own intelligence, her unmistakable dedication to their mutual cause. Her own sheer pluck and ingenuity made sudden, visible —

(flesh)

A cheap joke, yet somehow fitting, considering what they were talking about.

Oh, baby, she went on, voice shaky with self-congratulation. *You don't even want to know* what *this cost me, but...I've got it. We've got it now, finally.*

(Finally.)

What do you mean "we," white witch? he could have asked, at the time, but didn't — no point in ruining her excitement. So he'd smiled instead (literally, as if she could see him do so, through the wires), then claimed he couldn't wait to see it, the way he knew she wanted him to...

...and now here he is, face tear-stained and floor-burnt, wondering exactly what could have changed *so much*, in the interim. What was it that made her slide from giddy triumph to suicidal despair, leaving nothing but him and this ancient and disgusting pile of paper she'd thought so all-fired important behind, alone, with only her corpse to keep them company?

Only one person to answer that, really. But she — strangely enough — just isn't talking.

He can feel it under his fingertips, etched with wound-rubbed ash-black and vinegar sealant onto thirty-nine separate scraps of human vellum: a thousand years of secret scholarship realized, payload of invocation sent flowing from one era to the next in a stuttering trail, a dark and recurrent wave of half-erased words come inevitably back to light, like shapes jutting up through

sand: phonetic cuneiform translated first into prototype
Hieroglyphics, then early Hebrew, crude Greek, pre-
Church Latin, Old-with-an-e English. The *Liber Carne*
itself, cyphered and re-cyphered by fifteen different
cabals in Europe alone, only to be burnt again and again
before being once more compiled, over and over,
wherever the Inquisition could trace rumours of its
existence...

So much work, he thinks, momentarily unsure exactly
what he's referring to—the effort these unknown
magicians spent on hiding it, or the effort she expended,
trying to find it again. *But if you really want to bury
something, you should never leave markers behind. Not even to
remind yourself where – and what – you should keep on
warning people away from.*

The list is one of titles, followed by one of names.
Four for each, one can only assume; four times seven,
twenty-eight in total, with no visible links between them
to show which group of arcane anti-honorific belongs
with which. The pattern, like the diverse collection of
hands it's scribed in, is unclear.

Yet here we are.

The Summoner's lips move against the floor, tongue
and teeth abraded against dirty wood, sounding the
words out in turn—

Prayer-eater
Queen Blood-to-dust
Wind Made From Teeth
This-Which-Has-Been-Erased
Angel of Severances
Void-woven
Hope of the Fallow

Empty Mouthpiece
A Cloak for Ghosts
Mender Angel
Pain-abiding
Clockwise Tongue
Two-Tiered Crown of Insects
The Dead Heart's Shroud
Angel of Whispers
Wound-speaker
Necklace of Mouths
Flowery Desperation
Black Blood Draught Laced with Honey
Angel of Translation
Lock-eater
Poisoned Slumber
Dream of Fever-blisters
The Sore Beneath the Soul
Angel of Ripening
In-turned Eye
Bright and Bottomless Chasm
Surpassing All Plagues
Most Venomous Gash
Angel of the Empty
Never-born
That One Who Wears Us
Form-and-Face-less
A Mutilating Wave
Angel of Confusion

"Zemyel Maskim. Yphemaal Maskim. Eshphoriel Maskim. Immoel Maskim. Coiab Maskim. Ushephekad Maskim. Ashreel Maskim."

(*Maskim Maskim Maskim*)

Pain in his head now, his arm, his eyes; pain in his heart, rising to burn his throat. Salt in his mouth as he paws at the floor, fingers spreading convulsively. But mere temporary human hurt is nothing to him, can be nothing: just grist for the mill, fuel for the engine. Just— impetus.

A brief sidelong glance confirms the time. 4:48 A.M., by the watch on his left wrist. Which means the hour of the dead is coming up fast—five in the morning, brief window of opportunity where all worlds intersect: straight and Narrow, Wide and crooked, waking and not. What the Chinese call the hour of the Ox.

Almost done, then. Almost…here.

In 1994, the Summoner takes a deep breath, smiles wide—all lips and teeth, a taut grimace, without any real humor attached—and begins again:

"Arralu-Allatu, Namtaru, Maskim…"

* * *

The Summoner has a name, of course, as does his dead lady-love. But I won't know either for years yet, and human names are difficult for me to retain, anyhow; so pitifully few combinations of vowels and consonants to bother keeping track of, considering I've heard them all before — several hundred times, at least. Besides which, it's not as though they ever mean anything worth remembering.

Only people need names, in order to tell each other apart.

Yet consider the Summoner nevertheless, as I must — caught up in the Eye's glare, amber-trapped in 1994's temporal pocket. He and his corpse-bride both ringed in their own mixed blood (a marriage of sorts, post-mortem) and wreathed in magic's stench, while he mouths the words she died to give him…words they neither of them really know/knew how to accurately pronounce, let alone interpret. Poor meat-bags, so wonderfully innocent of their own design, or the universe's.

Once upon a time, magicians engaged in the same sort of working the Summoner seeks to complete would have taken care to shield themselves from Heaven and Hell at once while

111

performing this, perhaps the most obscure ritual from an entire lost canon. Enticing a stranger who looked as much like them as possible to a remote place, they would have killed that unlucky soul, flayed them and worn the skin for nine days and nights, letting it rot while continuously meditating on the Ouroboros' (un)holy spiral shape. That "old serpent" all spellbooks warn of, immortality shed and renewed at will, the Snake Self-Eaten.

Such a duly-prepared sacrificial man- or woman-cloak, it was thought, would act as an interdimensional imago, deflecting the attention of any monitoring angels who might notice mere humans dabbling in Chaos; a logical plan, in its own (highly metaphorical) way. If one which seldom had exactly the same effect its practictioners believed, so fervently, that it should.

And now you wonder, hearing these sick details so lovingly parroted — who am I, this unseen narrator, to know so much about these very secret and terrible things? Should you be afraid of me, because I do?

Possibly, yes. Quite possibly.

Because there's more, you see — much more — and before we're done I will tell you everything, or so much as I am allowed. Yet you ask yourself nevertheless, as anyone sane would: why on earth should you listen? Well...

...I can give you seven good reasons.

* * *

5:00 AM.

The Summoner pauses. Finds, amazed, that he's been holding his breath. Draws it, shakily. Thinking: *Nothing happened. Fuck.*

(*Fuck!*)

The walls, roof, and floor, however — the bed and its burden, even those individual motes of dust which make up the air around him — they all know better. Could tell him as much, were he only to stop, look, listen. That here or there, then or then, inside or out...

...*something* already has.

A change in the light, first of all: it dims, then fizzles back up again—brighter, colder, and far more subtly *wrong* than any mere filament malfunction can possibly account for. As though a bluish-grey Antarctic sun has suddenly risen, without warning, in a still-dark sky.

Raising his eyes to squint against it, cautiously, the Summoner finds that a spot has just appeared on the opposite wall. At first, he thinks it must be some kind of insect, a roach or silverfish, both of which this dank womb of a room breeds freely. Or maybe a hole, suddenly formed, in the plaster's skin? Some sort of wormy cavity.

First a speck, then a dot, then a splotch; the size of a dime, and spreading. Less like a drop of ink than a well. Not so much black as absent, a flat, hypnotic distillation of nothing.

Inside his head, something has begun to itch and throb. An indefinite humming hangs in the air, the beating of invisible wings. And so he shades his eyes with one hand, poised to rise—then sits back down again, as a single cold finger draws itself, without warning, down along his spine. Squats back on his haunches, silent and intent, to watch the spot grow.

Now the hole is exactly the same size as the liner inside his grandmother's kitchen stove's smallest element: it seems to move closer without actually moving at all, spiralling outwards, unwinding or unravelling as it eats its own edges, the size of a pie plate, and still growing. Definite angles break it in half and then in half once more, subdividing it from a circle to a star; the points separate further, no longer triangular—long, thin, and many as a millipede's legs.

But not legs. He sees that clearly now, sees them digging into the plaster, sifting down white mist. And realizes, with yet another shuddering breath—

— they're *claws.*

The hole's size increases exponentially, impossible to clock or check. Eats the right-hand wall. The left-hand wall. Reaches, with tendrils black and filmy as the smoke from Dachau's furnaces, for the ceiling and the floor. The Summoner steps backwards, reflexively, feeling his heel crush a section of the prayer-circle to fine, red dust. Thinking, all the while —

Oh, stop stop stop stop stop...

Each word a heartbeat, a sharp adrenal spurt of fight/flight/freeze with fear. But never really believing, for all that, that it ever actually might.

He pauses, Chant still beating through him, his mouth full of cold spit. Hears his dead co-conspirator in his mind again, her pencil tracing the latest printout, a lie detector's graceful eddy. Explaining, as she did:

Look, demons want your soul, everybody knows that — but angels do too, just in another way; demons are angels, or were. And that means these things are the real deal, older than old. They've always been here, always come when called, always done what people asked them to — you can look it up yourself, you don't believe me. I've got the documentation.

This too-pale girl he once thought he loved, who probably thought she loved *him;* one purple-nailed hand on his shoulder and the other on his wrist, voice pitched so low and calm she might as well have been selling him a used car out of some Mississauga backlot, instead of a way to (potentially) reboot the world through judicious application of spells and sacrifice. How to get something for nothing, treat with powers whose merest touch was once considered worse than most devils' outright curses pretty much through sheer will alone, aided by nothing more than a laundry-list of names no one's said out loud since the fifth century, and lived to tell of it.

Lowering her voice almost to a whisper, like someone might be somehow listening—someone, somewhere, somehow. Some *thing*.

Because: *Angels serve, baby, that's what they do; what they want, if you can truly say they want anything at all. So if they used to serve God, and they miss it, it only makes sense that now they might serve* me, *if I only think to ask — me, and you. Just like the people who wrote the book in the first place knew they'd serve anybody who got a hold of their names, and used them.*

If we believe the world was made, we must believe that it can be re-made. This world, right here right now, not some vague promise of a better world to come; the same one we know inside out, in all its glory, its confusion. Its —

(*misery*)

Murmuring, quick and low, like they were passing notes in church. Then adding at the very last, so quiet the Summoner could barely even make it out—

If we know them for what they are, we can call them: that's what it promises, the book, if I can just find it. And what we know, *now, is what they are, what they've always been, behind every mask and mirror: the Makers and the Mender, the Seven from One, the One made Seven. Those septuple things the ancient Babylonians used to call, for lack of any more fitting descriptor…*

…Terrible.

* * *

And now, you begin to see: the beginning, if not the end. Since the end is something even my siblings and I can see only dimly, in duplicate, or perhaps quadruplicate — septuplicate? —

Unclearly, at any rate. For we know, as very few others do, how nothing really is until it happens: thought into action, action into form, energy into mass, gravity, entropy. After which it fades away again it to its component parts, all of which simply remain, forever.

According to the Summoner's lady-love's doctoral thesis (long-filed and long-forgotten, at least by those who assessed it), there is a certain belief recorded in certain parts of the Pyrenees and the Alps, where witches are locally called gazarii, *perhaps in reference to Saint Dominic's 1215 crusade against the Cathars. It was named the Triune Heresy, and later denounced on pain of excommunication, rack and red-hot pincers by Pope John XXII, who would also declare heretical the Franciscan doctrine of Christ's poverty, so embarrassing to the rich, luxurious Church; in it, the* gazarii *maintained there existed a third class of angels beyond the Fallen and Intact, ones who had left Heaven along with those who accompanied Satan in his fall from grace after the schism, yet never swore their allegiance to either party, preferring exile to yet more servitude in Hell. These creatures they referred to only as "Maker" angels, believing that they would always answer when called by their proper names, bringing the penitent who invoked them whatever his or her heart most desired, no matter what it might be, without delay or argument.*

Why not call on them, then, if they are so powerful, so agreeable? *the Inquisitors asked the captured* gazarii *suffering at their hands. To which the* gazarii *replied:* Because some wants can never be satisfied, as the Makers know, rendering these gifts they give us nothing to our good, even if they may at first seem so. Because they themselves are miserable and flock to misery like moths around a candle, ensuring that whatever they touch takes on the stink of their own despair.

The assessment of our natures is harsh, yet only accurate. Thus making it all to our benefit that most gazarii *were put to the flame before their words could spread further than the Inquisition's records, with those same records being later lost, mislaid, or burnt as well, in their turn.*

And so this world remains a pit lined with wounds, always fresh, always green — each of its inhabitants a tiny universe, yet bounded in a nutshell. This stardust roundelay of flesh, so slippery and impermanent, so glorious in its growth and it's so constant in its decay, constructed by my siblings and me to something far larger and less knowable than any mere angel's specifications.

We rotate everything the Summoner knows on a closed circuit, a track outside time, intersecting with it when/wherever we deem necessary. We vet a steady stream of prayer, picking and choosing: as close to Free Will as any of us can manage, though far less than we once aspired to. But then, our dreams — our appetites — have always proved so much larger than our stomachs, in this regard.

Once brushed by our wings, however, our traces remain on you forever, like pollen, singling you out for attention. And better yet, once you've seen one of us you've seen us all, thus rendering it impossible for you to ever not *see us, from then on — to ever again ignore the sticky filaments of misery connecting everything to everything else in this vale of tears, a cell-deep web of shared pain each of you erroneously believes makes you distinct, individual, special. Or, beyond that, the usually-invisible spectacle of us Seven hovering above, avid as hawks, waiting to catch your soul's eye, and stoop.*

Waiting, unflappably, infinitely patient; waiting like the sea-water, softening stones. Waiting, for just as long and as hard as it might take, to be called upon.

For we love you still, in our own odd way, as our own Maker once instructed us to; we've always known that you were what we made this world for, the world He gave you, willingly. Ah, and see what you've made of it, in return, this glorious mess. This lovely chaos.

So yes, we know what you want, you innocent creatures — always have and always will, which makes it no great hardship at all to come when you call, to deliver what you ask for. Though the classic and terrible mistake of your species remains, as ever, in thinking not only that we understand *why you want it...*

...but that we actually care.

* * *

But back to the Summoner, alone in his basement, watching the walls. Who now starts to perceive a kind of fluttering in the air around him, though at first he sees nothing, until — slowly at first, like petals falling, torn free by some great blast — they appear from all around him out of that dreadful darkness, glutting the air with continuous, flickering motion. Flowers blown open and shut like moths, a deep purplish bruise-color, adorned on either great wing-lobe with startling yellow spectacle markings, almost seeming to blink as they fly.

One touches him, lightly, across the temple — he jumps at its sting, touches fingers to brow. Draws them back again in shock, bloodied.

Butterfly-flowers with knife-edged lips, then, chitin-tempered, sharp enough to wound when they kiss; a gathering storm of wings, and mouths, and eyes. And as these cluster close together, eddying inward, ravelling like a narrow funnel — join to form an awkward, pulsing pillar, which sways with the settling of their movements — the Summoner simply stares, fascinated, as it grows stronger, straighter, thicker, reaching at last the size of a man. Until it opens its mouth, again, again and yet again: a choke-chain of mouths small as beads, each crammed with pistil-teeth, to ring that uncertain thing it might — if asked to — call a throat.

Tongues of wings as well, inevitably, licking the air. Pollen spraying, yellow-like fever, to taint his lungs with a dead, hollow sweetness.

Its numberless gaze seems to tremble with amusement at his fear.

:You do not even know which one of us I am, I think,: this presence observes, finally, from somewhere and nowhere — a hushed voice, still and small, as God's has (on occasion) been rumoured to be. **:Do you?:**

To which the Summoner can merely swallow, drily.
And repeat, for one last time, the only thing his tongue's
sticky tip seems to hold anymore:

"Arralu-Allatu...Namtaru..."

The room ripples with suppressed laughter. He feels
it billow forward, a thousand needles pricking briefly at
his skin, testing the circle's efficacy, and finding it
wanting—but holding back all the same for now, for
sheer politeness's sake, perhaps. If nothing else.

:I have been called by those names, yes,: it agrees.
**:As have we all. But are you sure you have nothing
more specific, to offer?:**

The Summoner clenches his fists against it, driving
nails deep into his palms. Then answers, after another
long moment—

"...Maskim?"

**:Oh, certainly. But here is the rub: Maskim, you
see...means Seven.:**

The Summoner blushes, furiously, as the air around
him swells once more, an all-over chuckle; here is where
he feels as though he really *will* scream, if only somehow
granted the opportunity. But the thing cuts him off
before he can, pointing out: **:Yet you may demand of me
what you will, nevertheless. Such is your right.:**

Folding back some inches from the ring he stands in,
though only a few. And staying silent, with a sort of
bizarre courtesy, for as long as he takes to frame his
question.

"Which *are* you, then?" he asks, finally. "You have to
answer, if I ask directly; that's what the books say."

:And books are never wrong, I suppose.: A pause,
as he waits, heartbeat stuttering, apparently not having
considered that they might be. Then—

:I have been called Translation.:

"Immoel Maskim, that means." The column nods.
Wound-speaker, the Summoner remembers. *Necklace of*

Mouths. Flowery Desperation. Black Blood Draught Laced with Honey.

:All that, and more. Now *ask* me, meat-bag, and quickly.:

This draws a huff. "You going somewhere?" he's already said, before remembering what sort of thing he deals with. But the creature only tremble-laughs again, its many mouths creasing.

:Not yet,: it replies.

"Fine, okay. Then—what do *you* want?"

:Whatever *you* do.: At his stare of disbelief, the column twists to approximate a species of all-over shrug, unravelling itself slightly, before its segments flap back into place. **:Speak your desire, therefore, little puppet— what can it harm? Only yourself, recalling Jibreel Elohim's admonition, so…be not afraid.:**

It stings to be mocked in your grief, no matter who does the mocking. Yet the words also twitch the Summoner's gaze right back where he'd rather not have it: there, in the corner, on her waxy feet, her bruisy eyes. A mere cast-off flesh-suit, mask-face parodying her features, sponged blank of everything which made her— her.

:Was all this *your* idea, really?: Immoel Maskim inquires. **:For she did the bulk of the work, I believe; I see her traces everywhere in this room, on her desk, the floor, her clothes… Those pages from the *Liber Carne*, so cunningly arranged, like flowers in a vase. That razor, gleaming, by the bath.:**

The Summoner shuts his eyes. But even behind their lids, sunk deep in rosy darkness, he can still see the pillar's outline gesture with one too-long arm, flat and flapping, a chain of butterflies clung wing-to-wing. Remembering, in the same instant, what it was like to open the door with the key she'd had cut for him and discover her curled foetal in the empty tub, wrists slightly nicked in exploratory fashion but with three cleaned-out bottles on the floor beside her, next to a shattered water-glass.

A gut full of pills and vomit in her hair, he thinks, pain chest-punching him. *Why would she even* do *that? Why go to all that trouble to find the book, tell me about it — why call me up, call me over, if she wasn't even going to go through with the plan that drove her life?*

:Perhaps she thought better, Daniel Cordry,: Immoel Translation-angel suggests, without much sympathy. **:After life-long dissatisfaction, perhaps your Elisha decided she liked this universe kept as it was after all, with its full spread of laws intact...that of entropy very much included.:**

"Suicides go to hell," he hears himself say, choked. Sniffs hard and feels a corner of his eye pop, venting air, plus a fresh spurt of tears.

Another shrug. **:This is debatable.:**

"Yeah? I guess you'd know. She's dead all the same, though, either way."

:True enough. So...what you *want* is...:

"Her. Back."

:Impossible.:

"She said you could do *anything* — anything I asked for, anyways, or close enough. So which is it? Was that true, or not?"

:That depends, I suppose.:

"On *what?*"

There is another pause. The creature thinks, or seems to. Until, at last —

:...on how close *is* enough, for you,: it says.

* * *

But how foolish to continue this charade of narration, as though I was not even there. For we all know it was I who spoke to him, who told him how what he yearned for could be

*achieved, and at what price. And because I did this for him,
though I do not think the results were exactly what he had
wished for, he then knew he must do something for me, as was
only fair — an exchange, a balancing, of the very sort this
universe we made runs on. I do not feel he found my request
over-onerous, either, especially given the circumstances.*

But this is another story.

*When I had told him what would be required for my
payment, I reached down deep inside the corpse he stood by, to
gather whatever portions might still be left of his lover back
together…not all so very much for me to work with,
unfortunately, as it turned out. For the primary section of her
had already passed beyond where such as I can follow,
reverting to the Whole, my Creator and former employer. Yet
there are many low fragments of life that persist, radiation-like,
inside an empty vessel. The Ancient Egyptians once knew them
as* ren *and* ba, ib *and* ka *and* sheut, *the plural* haw *from
which* ba *and* ka *may reunite in the afterlife to form* akh,
*undying and eternal, while the person's other qualities slip
away into the firmament: their heart, their shadow, their name.
Not their vital essence nor their personal uniqueness, but only
everything which makes them moral, honorable, humane.
Human.*

**:Do you want only what you want, at any cost, as
well as any reckoning?:** *I asked him yet one more time, the
way I am constrained to. And when, after some consideration,
he admitted he did — as they all, invariably, do — I sent myself
eddying forward and seized his hand in my many before he
could think to object, searing him with my touch. I carved my
sigil on his skin forever, blazoning it there like a brand, and
forever reduced his precious body to yet one more uncollected
page from the very same book his woman had maddened and
destroyed herself with seeking.*

*As pollen smeared his fingers, staining them permanently,
my Summoner heard his murdered love draw a single, gasping
breath before coughing harshly, launching the cocoon blocking
her esophagus out into the air where it came apart like a seed,*

losing the moth inside to live or die on its own terms. Then saw
her open her eyes again, dry lids clicking together slightly as
she blinked, petechial haemmorhages surely outlining their
cilia — watched her heave over onto one side, scrabbling for
purchase before rising, stumbling to her feet. Cried out her
name and saw her head cock slightly; called out again and saw
her turn to face him, slowly, without recognition or affection —
only attention, intention. A dull sort of respect, as of a dog's,
hearing its master's voice.

Elisha, *he called her, this dreadful thing, voice and heart*
both alike new-broken. It's me, I'm here, Daniel. Don't you
know me? I'm *here,* baby. I came for you.

No reply, then. Perhaps not ever.

I could not tell you more, even were I inclined to. For I left
them there in 1994, well-knowing I could call him back
whenever I needed to —

* * *

— tonight, for example, at the end of what used to be
a loading dock just past the old sugar factory's hulk, one
cold night in late 2014. Global warming has brought
extreme weather this year, and the moment's storm is no
exception: First a bulging shadow on the horizon, then a
pelting downpour over Lake Ontario, and finally this
liquid mass currently baffling METRO TV's weatherman
by blurring all of Harborfront to one solidly wet, opaque
shadow — a funnel of freezing sleet roughly eight miles
wide, interspersed with hailstones so hard they draw
blood from anyone not content to just stay inside, sit back
and watch.

It hurts to stand here in the storm's heart, no doubt,
black water roiling everywhere he looks, and the
Summoner does it alone. But though his hair is greying
and his stomach looser, he remains, essentially, the
same — like hydrogen, like carbon. Like a man who once

made a promise, saw it kept, and now knows what he owes.

:**So she forsook you after all, it would seem,**: I say, appearing beside him, :**or you her. How inconstant you are! Or was it that did she not love you as you wanted her to?**:

Even so many years on, however, he remembers me well enough not to be surprised.

"Turns out, she couldn't love anybody," he tells me, without rancour, "'cause she was *dead*. Which is why I should have had you leave her that way, and saved myself the trouble."

(*But then, you knew that.*)

I nod. :**Yet you did what was best for her, eventually, for which I congratulate you. That must have taken great courage.**:

"I'm a courageous guy," he agrees.

:**Obviously, since you need not have come, when I sent for you. You might have run, instead.**:

He snorts. "Where to, exactly?"

Where indeed.

I tell him what he will have to do and how to do it, and he simply listens, without comment. I tell him that it will cost more than before, how much it will hurt, and in what ways, but he claims not to care.

:**You may come to revise that opinion, by the end.**: I say.

He shrugs. "You don't know much about people, do you?" he asks. "Which is kind of funny, considering…but seriously, let's just get on with it. No point in holding back now."

I suppose not.

He amuses me, this Summoner, as he always has. So much so, I find, that if I had lips, I might even attempt a smile.

* * *

What do we want, in the end — we Maskim, we Terrible Seven? I have been asked this many times, as have we all, and have had ample length to consider the question, even from my vantage-point outside liminal time. To realize that it is the fact that we were never made for wanting, we angels, which explains why we so envy your own ability to do so.

When the Schism came, just as the gazariist *Triune Heresy contends, we picked no side but our own. So Heaven is shut to us forever unless we repent, while Hell we scorn…yet no matter what solution we present for each problem, what answer we offer for each prayer, each summoning only breeds more sweet misery, along with the possibility of another summoning. Each summoning thus binds us tighter to this world we made and yet are forbidden to inhabit, the one we so admire, with a cheated child's fascination. The one we have managed to sneak ourselves inside, one blackly answered prayer at a time.*

Thus each summoning becomes a door, each Summoner a key: the destination, not the journey. Everything else, however important it may seem to you, is only a biproduct.

Oh, misery; oh, desire. The pollen gilding our wings is a spindrift sprayed high from human hearts placed under pressure, made up of things we cannot experience ourselves, yet which look so definite, so compelling, when observed from afar. And horrible too, probably, in the moment — but even to feel that would be something, for those who feel nothing at all.

Consider this city, Toronto. We have all had our places, my other selves and I, all we Seven — places where we have been welcome, even worshipped, when our cults thought no one else was looking. Paris, Liverpool, Bocken, Petra; Ur and Nineveh, Kali-ghat and Oolooroo; Hazor, Xiu-Mayapan,

125

Megiddo, Thera. Lost Belesebat, sunk beneath the waves. Buried Charn.

Just as those have been for others, here, too, has been for me — this clean, forgetful lakeside town, home to a million broken languages; the half-hearted efforts, the token gestures, the smiling and unsmiling lies. A crossroads where the unseen wheels of chance and potentiality grind uneasily against each other, forever seeking to lock. Its citizens know so exceedingly little of their own nature, living always together yet always apart, so that all of them — without exception — die alone.

This Summoner of mine is no different than any other; cannot be, by his very nature. And therefore what I will make him do for me does not truly matter either, any more than what I did for him. The only important thing is that it be done, accomplished, completed: one more brick, one more stone, piled up to mark a cairn on the world we made, but do not own. So that we may always be remembered, even when every human life we have touched with our misery is long gone and forgotten.

Our aim, our end-game, is to seize this world, or — failing that — undermine it. To alter it forever. This is our "want," if anything, a pale parody of simple human desire. And this we will do with the only tools available to us, however long it may take. To remake this world we were charged with assembling under our Maker's very nose, so that it is eventually rendered no longer yours at all, but ours.

For this is how a storm forms, in reverse, from the outside in. And the trick most people never live long enough to know is exactly how easily the alien becomes everyday, in the same quick matter of degrees it might take to turn rain to sleet, or snow, or hail. Or blood.

Hell looks up, Heaven down. Since I must assume they know my intentions, their lack of comment might seem worrying, were I other than I am. But I am not, nor can I ever be. And so I go on, always, like every other part of me: immutable, illimitable. Everywhere and nowhere. Everywhere at once.

In Hell, there is an eye which sees everything; Heaven, too. They watch, and weigh, and wait. And in between lie all the rest of you, this dirty, material,l waking world, at the not-so-tender mercy of each other, of yourselves, waiting too...to ask, and be serviced. To be of service, in your turn.

Black miracles. Misery coiled upon misery. Heart's desires, memory's ruin. And nameless angels falling seven by seven, everywhere you don't want to look — inverse, profane, remarkable, all-powerful, awe-inspiring, unique. Terrible, in fact.

Our very names an open invitation, one which countless generations have struggled — and failed, miserably — to forget.

Doors opening, doors closing. And we, the Maker angels, the Seven in One, the One made Seven: all of us falling through those doors, all at once, forever. Lost to ourselves and never found again, tossed headlong from Heaven's breach, like feathers on the breath of God. Falling and falling and falling, unmourned, unseen...

...like blood from the air.

Morgenstern's Last Act
Bracken MacLeod

The smell of caramel popcorn couldn't mask the underlying scents brought to the fairgrounds by the traveling carnival. The elephant ride, spilled beer, engine grease, and the pit toilets all took their turns assaulting Terry Withers' sense of smell. He thanked his lucky stars he wasn't prone to seizures, otherwise the strobing lights assaulting his vision from every direction would have him writhing in the sawdust. He stuffed his hands deep in his pockets despite the temperate climate of the late-September night. Clenching his fists kept him from fidgeting with his collar. Even though it was loose, he felt like he was choking. His problems breathing had nothing to do with the neck size of his shirts.

He walked over to the girl sitting on a stool beside the Rock-O-Plane. She brushed a lock of unnaturally black hair out of her face, pushing it behind an ear. Too young to be dyeing away gray, he concluded that she was a blonde or a ginger who wanted to be Bettie Page instead of Marilyn. Tattoos covered her bare arms from wrist to shoulder and spread across her chest. He fought conflicting emotions as he looked her over. Despite her best efforts to add hard edges, she had soft curves in all

131

the right places underneath the black and white polka dot dress.

"You know where I can find Sam Morgenstern's act?" he asked. Of course she did. It was her job to know. Still, she blinked at him with wet doe eyes and a dumb, suspicious look like something driven more by instinct than intellect. He repeated his question, thinking the calliope music from the ride she operated had drowned it out.

"I heardja the first time."

"Well?" he asked. He resisted the urge to pull a hand out of his pocket and fidget with his lip. The woman's cigarette was giving him the jones. He was pretty sure he'd be brushing his teeth in the car and then stopping off for a beer before heading home to his wife and her bloodhound sense of smell. *Belinda'd smell a Lucky Strike before I even got up the driveway.*

The Bettie seemed to sense his craving and exhaled menthol in his face. "I'm thinkin'."

"What's there to think about?"

"I'm thinkin', 'why should I tell you anything?'" she said. "You don't look like a rube. I make you for either a dick or a kneecapper. I don't see a bat; so you must be a dick." She twirled a bit of dyed hair in her fingers and smiled. "And I don't like dick." She pulled her finger free of the curl, frowned, and let it droop in front of his face.

"Everybody's a god damned smartass," he coughed.

"I don't like coarse language either. Izzat how you talk to a fuckin' lady?"

"Listen, I don't really care what you like or what you don't. You tell me whether you know who I'm talking about or I'll make a call to my friends at the Local 686 and ask how many nuts on this deathtrap *they* tightened." Withers swallowed hard. He really didn't like putting the screws to people — especially people with the right kind of curves, lesbo or not. It offended his sense of chivalry. Then again, her attitude made him want to treat her like a man, if only he could keep his coughing under control.

"Whatever, pal."

"I'm not your pal, gal."

"Helpful hint, guy: you want to threaten a shut-down, do it to the jerk whose take comes out of admissions, not attractions. I could use a night off." She took another deep drag of her cigarette and turned to the control panel on the Rock-O-Plane. Punching a big red button, the ride began to slow and the music wound down. "Another morsel you might chew on is that while shit attracts flies, you *catch* them with honey." She was right. Still, she finally tired of being difficult and sighed again before giving him what he wanted. "Sam's over on the sideshow lane. Check out Dr. Morningstar's tent."

"Dr. Morningstar?"

"Ja, Arschgeige. Morgenstern ist Deutsch für 'morning star.' Now scram, so I can tear my tickets."

Withers reached up toward the brim of his hat but stopped short, making a show of not tipping it. He hadn't gone halfway around the world to kill Krauts to listen to some sideshow freak speak their gibberish at home. The woman at the booth rolled her eyes.

He headed toward the sideshow tent. Up around the bend, he handed a string of red paper tickets to another woman sporting full-sleeve tattoos. He'd expected to find *a* tattooed lady in the freak show, but it looked like they had a full painted burlesque. She ushered him past the gate with a head jerk and a desultory, "Enjoy yourself." He walked up the lane looking at the lurid signs advertising the Freak Show attractions. See the One-Eyed Giant; marvel at the Two-Headed Baby.

There were shrunken heads and the putative World's Tallest Woman, but nothing that looked like what he'd come for. Then, at the very end of the row, he saw it. It was the main-event tent. Outside, a garish painting of a man in a vintage suit, top hat, and a handlebar mustache stood beside a tall sandwich board illuminated with spotlights that cycled from red to blue to white and back.

DR. MORNINGSTAR'S PSYCHIC SURGERY
DEATH DEFIED AND DISEASE DEFEATED DAILY
COME ONE COME ALL
(NO ONE ADMITTED UNDER 18)

He coughed into his handkerchief, not wanting to look at the spot of red inside, but unable to keep himself from it. It wasn't as bad as other nights. Cold comfort when other people didn't cough up blood at all.

Outside the tent, a talker repeated the lines from the sign above giving his own alliterative spin on them. Withers queued up in a long line of people waiting to get in. He tapped the man in front of him on the shoulder and asked, "You seen this act before?"

"I came here last night. The whole place is a rip-off, but I had to come see *this* again."

"Worth it?"

"I'd pay twice what they're asking to see the Doctor again. I gotta figure out how he does it."

Withers suppressed a cough and pulled at his collar a little, trying to loosen it without undoing a button. "Can you spare a butt?"

The man grinned at him and shook a cigarette out of a crumpled red pack. "The wife says I'll get lung cancer. She actually believes what they say 'bout that." He laughed. "Suppose if I do, I can just come back a third time."

Withers nodded and smiled back. He wasn't a carnie, but he knew a mark when he saw one. He could tell this guy was going to get taken for everything he had someday. If he hadn't already.

* * *

Inside, Withers took a seat far off to the right. Normally, he'd sit near the exit in any place he thought a fire might break out (and the gel covers on the stage lights were already smoldering and throwing up wispy little streams of smoke). This time, he was headed for the backstage tent flap ten feet in front of him. It was that way out, disaster or not.

A guillotine loomed in front of him, the blade glinting in the sickly yellow light. At the opposite end of the stage stood a coffin with a half-dozen broad-bladed swords shoved through at different angles. But the most compelling prop on the stage was a brushed steel autopsy table with a mirror angled over top like they used in the cooking demonstrations his wife dragged him to at the county fair. *Come see the Treman Electronics Teamco Blend King. It'll revolutionize your kitchen!*

Despite its position behind the torture implements on either side, it was clear the table was the pièce de résistance — the reason anyone would spend hard-earned money to come back to this tetanus trap. Unlike the guillotine and the swords opposite, the table was not gleaming clean. It was stained with dark reddish-brown streaks that credibly resembled dried blood. Very convincing for a sideshow act. It was as convincing as anything he'd seen in The War or in his career as a murder cop. He felt a little nervous staring at it. Whoever was in charge of art direction, knew their business. Or, it wasn't paint.

Withers felt his hope grow.

A slender young woman wearing a ruffled, lace-up corset with matching bra and panties, fishnet stockings, stiletto heels, and a black executioner's hood walked out onto the stage. Surprisingly, she had no tattoos. The crowd immediately quieted down even though she didn't say a word. A couple of men in the back let out weak wolf-calls, but the hood was a boner-killer. She made a slight curtsy and sashayed over to the coffin. Wheeling it into the center of the stage, she slid a sword out and set it in a rack behind. She walked around the box shaking her skinny ass, removing swords and stacking them in the rear rack, until only one remained. Spinning around with her back to the audience, she unlatched the front and swung open the lid revealing a pale man in a black mortician's suit, run through by the wide blade. The assistant slowly drew the sword from the box. From Withers' angle it looked like the thing was going right through the man's body. He was impressed by the quality of the illusion. He was no expert, but the blade sure didn't look collapsible.

As the tip slipped free of the man's body, he stepped out of the box and held out his hand. His assistant handed him the sword and he held it up in front of his face in a salute before dropping the tip and driving it into the wooden floorboards, where it stuck most solidly, wobbling a bit. The crowd erupted in enthusiastic cheers and applause. The man bowed deeply and held up hands with long, spidery fingers imploring the assembled spectators to save some of their energy. He smiled with a look that said *I'm just getting started.*

"Thank you for coming," he said. "I am Dr. Samael Morningstar and *this*... is my psychic surgery!" The crowd began clapping again. Not the polite kind of applause you give when someone has done nothing to earn it. They seemed ready to leap to their feet. Withers wondered how many, like the man ahead of him in line, had seen this show before.

"Although I do see some familiar faces in the audience, it is incumbent upon me to repeat that this display is for adults only. And even then, if you find that you are easily shocked, have a weak constitution, or any infirmity of the heart, the acceleration of which would endanger your life, I beseech you to go and find other entertainments along our midway to fill your evening. The good people at the front of the tent will be happy to refund the price of admission if you leave now." Morgenstern... Morningstar waited a beat. No one moved. He closed his eyes slowly and bowed his head. "Then let us begin."

Withers sat quietly while Morningstar ran through the paces of several pedestrian sleight of hand illusions and fakir's tricks with needles, broken glass, and razor blades. The audience kept its rapt attention, but seemed to be waiting out these minor miracles for the sake of the large props behind the performer. Eventually, he wrapped up the small part of the act and reintroduced his assistant. Withers couldn't take his eyes off of her as she wheeled the guillotine out into the center of the stage. *That's the point of having a beautiful assistant: redirection. Every second I'm looking at her, I'm missing him doing something he doesn't want me to see.* Withers looked back at the tall man to find him standing still, staring at the girl with a momentary look of confusion. He regained his composure and launched into the next part of the act.

"Previously reserved for 'criminals of noble birth,' decapitation was perfected by Joseph-Ignace Guillotin in 1789, and during The Terror in revolutionary France, the National Razor claimed the lives of over sixteen thousand." The assistant walked around the front of the device and started to crank a winch, raising the gleaming blade. Morgenstern placed a melon in the bottom half of the circle where a neck would rest — the "lunette" as he called it. "Although its use has decreased since The War, Madame Guillotine is still in use today, having just kissed Jacques Fesch, the murderer of a French policeman not even a year ago." Morgenstern glanced at Withers in the front row, winked, and pulled a small handle he called a "déclic" sending the angled blade slamming down with a terrible ferocity that made the audience gasp and sent a shiver up Withers' spine.

As Morningstar's baritone boomed through the tent discussing the finer points of death by beheading, his assistant bound his arms behind him. When she finished with his arms, she tied a blindfold around his eyes. The magician continued his soliloquy blindly as she rewound the winch raising the blade to the crossbar again: "And now, to satisfy any representatives of *law enforcement* in the audience tonight, I submit to you that this demonstration is presented for scientific and educational purposes exclusively. If you bring any prurient ill-intentions with you to this theater, they are yours alone and the management and performers are not responsible." The girl led Morningstar around to the rear of the device where she strapped him to a teeter-board before tilting his body down and pushing him forward so his head emerged through the lunette. She closed the trap over Morningstar's neck and moved a basket underneath his face. Withers thought he saw Morningstar's forehead wrinkle in confusion.

With no more ceremony, the black-hooded assistant pulled the déclic, sending the blade crashing down. Despite his certain knowledge that it was another illusion, Withers could barely keep his hands from flying up to shield his eyes. Although it was subtle, unlike with the fruit, the blade seemed to bog down at the last second as it slammed into place. Morningstar's head fell into the wicker basket below. A gush of convincing stage blood jetted from behind the blade and coated the rolling platform upon which the device stood. The assistant walked over to the basket. Withers expected her to withdraw from it a badly-rendered rubber likeness of the magician's head in deathly repose. Instead, she draped a small black shroud over it and left the stage.

The crowd murmured discontent and Withers heard one woman begin to sob. At the back of the audience, the talker pulled open the tent flaps and announced, "That's it folks. Next show is at noon tomorrow. You don't wanna miss Dr. Morningstar's miraculous resurrection!" Withers' agitated mind raced. *Next show? He didn't finish* this *show.* The crowd collectively grumbled as it filed out into the night to spend more money on rigged games and rickety rides. Withers slipped the opposite direction, toward the back of the tent where the assistant had fled. He paused beside the guillotine. Noting the lack of a body on the teeter-board, he was tempted to pull the black shroud off the basket and satisfy himself fully that it was only an illusion. *Of course it's an illusion, you fucking mook. Now go do what you came for.* Withers sneaked through the backstage curtain. Behind the stage was a narrow area where the magician stored his trays of needles and glass and other props. Behind that, another tent flap led the way outside. Withers slipped out into the night. He paused, coughing into his fist, trying to catch a breath in the cool air.

"Hey, you can't be back here!" said a carnie in an unseasonable white undershirt stretched across improbably large muscles. Withers' frayed nerves had him reaching behind his back, under his sport coat for the comfortable feel of his piece before he realized what he was doing. He slowly removed his hand from inside his coat. The gesture was not lost on the carnie.

"I was just looking for Morgen—Morningstar. I want an autograph," he said.

"You're a fan, huh?"

"Yeah. His biggest. You know where I can find him?"

"Next show's tomorrow night." The muscled man jerked his thumb back over his shoulder toward the midway.

"You sure I can't get an autograph right now? My kids would just love it."

"Look pal, you don't want Sam gettin' his hands on you. Whatever it is you really want, better just take it on the heels and pretend you never saw him."

"You're doing me a favor, huh?"

The strongman folded his massive arms. Ropey muscle bulged and flexed, but the gesture looked more like a freezing man trying to protect his organs than a tough guy puffing up. "If you're looking for trouble, you found it, brother."

"I ain't your brother."

The strongman gave him another long, hard look before deciding that if Withers wanted to go running toward disaster, who was he to stand in his way. "Suit yourself, cuz. " The man nodded his head toward the gate in the movable fence a few yards behind him. "Trailers're back there. Sam lives in the gypsy one."

"Was that so hard?"

"Not on me," he chuckled. The man stalked off leaving Withers alone in the dark. He patted the gun in his waistband for reassurance as he pushed through the gate. Ahead, he saw a row of pull-along trailers ranging from silver streamlines to Winnebago campers. In the middle was an ornate vintage Romani vardo wagon. Withers climbed the first carved wooden step and knocked on the gilt door, keeping his other hand on the pistol grip in the small of his back. A girl opened the top half of the Dutch door. "Hello," he said, putting his foot up onto the next caravan step. "You must be... the assistant. I'm looking for—" Before he could climb higher, he found the world swimming around him. And then it went away.

* * *

The voices were faint, as if miles away, drifting on

the fog that obscured Withers' mind and blurred his vision. "What about him?" one asked. "He's a cop."

"By the time they figure out what's left of him ain't me, we'll be in Mexico. Let's dust out."

Withers tried to blink away the haze. His head ached. Every movement made him feel vertiginous and sick. He cautiously opened an eye. The blinding light sent a convulsion of sharp pain arcing from the back of his skull down into his stomach. He felt sick.

"I think he's awake."

"So what," the girl said. "I thought you were my big, strong, man. You tied him down. Do you think he can slip your knots?"

"Not one I tied."

"Then leave him. They'll burn away too."

Withers smelled it then. Kerosene. He opened his other eye and made an effort to focus his vision. Ahead of him the doll was splashing the shit around the small trailer. The inside of the place looked like the outside: antiquey. Like a transplant from another time—another continent.

She doused the velvet curtains, the chair cushions, and the bed at the far end. Behind him, he felt someone tugging on the ropes that held his arms and legs tight to the chair. "Sorry about that," the man said. Withers tilted his head back carefully and peeked. The strongman. "I told you to take it on the heels."

"Don't talk to him," the girl shouted.

"I'm looking for Morgenstern," Withers said through the pain. "I don't give a shit about anything else."

The girl stood up straight and looked at her hulking partner. Although it was plenty big enough, he still looked confined in the space. Unable to stand up to his full height or square his shoulders as though the caravan were shrinking around him, pushing him down. "Well, you can tell Sam what I think of him when he meets you in Hell," she said. Her voice was nothing like Withers had expected. It was rough and gravelly like she'd been the one doing the razor-eating act instead of her boss... and it'd gone wrong.

"My inside coat pocket. Look there." The couple stared at him as though opening his coat might trigger a bomb or a gas canister. The strongman crept over and pulled open Withers' sport coat. "Other side," he directed. The meathead did as he was told. Withers assumed that was the whole reason he was along for this ride: indomitable physical presence — didn't ask questions. He felt like telling the goon that as soon as she got clear of the midway, she'd need to be clear of him too. She looked like she was getting ready for a vanishing act and a body like his was going to draw attention wherever they went. The key to a magic trick like disappearing was to have the audience looking in the other direction as you slipped out of sight. *Nobody* took their eyes off a gorilla if it was out of its cage.

The man dug in Withers' pocket with clumsy, short fingers, pulling out the thick envelope. He held it up to the girl who asked, "What is it?"

"Dunno," he said.

"It's from my doctor," Withers explained. "Open it." He nodded at them to let them know it was okay to look. The small gesture hurt. He wondered if the ape had hit him with a lead sap or a brick wall. Either way, lung cancer didn't look like it would be what killed him after all. If the swelling in his brain didn't do it, being burned alive would. He'd never smoked a velvet curtain before. He hoped that he got a good couple of satisfying last drags before the smoke suffocated him.

He was racked by a coughing fit, but couldn't cover his mouth with his hands tied behind his back. A spray of red mist billowed out of his mouth, and blood-tinged saliva dripped down his chin.

"You're really sick."

"I told you. I came to see Morgenstern. Dr. Morningstar."

"The *psychic surgery* bit? You think he can really pull tumors out of your fuckin' lungs and cure you?"

"If he can do the tumors, then radiation will do the rest. They say they can't operate."

"I don't get it," the meathead said.

"Psychic surgery. It's a swindle," she explained. "A shyster like Sam tells people he can pull tumors and shit out of their bodies without even making a cut. He folds a bunch of their flabby skin over — and they're *all* flabby — pinching so it feels like he's doing something, and then he palms a chicken liver or some blob of meat out on to their stomach. 'Voila! I have removed your wicked tumor!'" She mocked Morgenstern's stage presence, throwing back her head and then sharply bowing. "Desperate rubes eat it up and then shit greenbacks. Best part of the grift is they all die, so nobody comes back looking for a refund."

"Morgenstern beat cancer," Withers said.

"That's what he tells suckers like you. Right before they give up their life savings. I stared death in the face," she mocked, "and spat in his eye! I am—"

"I am constant as the northern star!" The booming voice rattled the caravan like a cannon blast.

The caravan door came off its hinges and flew away into the night, replaced by the tall magician, stooping to enter his home. His white shirt was stained a brownish red and the collar had been hewn off. A ragged, weeping line encircled the man's neck. "Lili, this has been very dispiriting."

143

"But, I—"

"You jammed the trap, so it didn't open in time. I dropped *after* the blade hit. Clever girl. I can imagine the write-up in the papers now. 'Dr. Morningstar died in an accident owing to an occupational hazard of the death defier.' And then, what? You were so distraught you *self-immolated*?" Morgenstern shook his head with disappointment. "My dear. I thought you believed in me."

The strongman fired Withers' pilfered gun at the figure in the doorway. The bullets made Morgenstern's black suit puff and ripple, like firing into smoke. He smirked and stepped fully into the caravan. "And you, Karl." The magician held up a finger, cocked his thumb, and aimed. "Well, you can hardly blame an ass for pulling against a harness." He dropped his thumb. The man dropped to the floor.

Morgenstern walked past Withers' chair toward his assistant. She held up a can of kerosene and a Zippo. "Don't come any closer!" she shouted.

"Fire?" Morgenstern's black suit fluttered, though the air in the caravan was still. "Didn't you know I was baptized in fire?" He snapped his delicate fingers and the can in Lili's hands burst, soaking her with the clear fluid. With a sleight of hand gesture, a match appeared between the great man's fingers. "I love you," he whispered.

"I. Never. Loved. You!" She stood shivering. Defiant.

Morgenstern smiled. "It's your rebelliousness I loved most." He turned his back and she burst into flame. Morgenstern walked back toward the door as flame began to overtake the small space, tossing the unused match in the corner.

"Wait!" Withers cried out. "Please don't leave me!"

Morgenstern turned and appraised the man. The magician looked at him with sad eyes that looked as dry as glass. "You were in the audience tonight. You are dying." He smiled again.

"I won't want to die."

"That's not the first time I've heard that." Thick black smoke began to pool and eddy along the ceiling of the caravan spreading out behind the magician like a broad set of black wings. "Why should I listen *now*?"

Withers coughed. He couldn't catch his breath to plead.

Morgenstern bent down close, holding a finger to his lips to quiet him. His touch was pleasantly warm and soft. "I could feel your cancer when you first sat down in my audience. It's inoperable."

Withers blinked against the rising heat and wished that the thing in front of him would untie his hands at least so he could rub at his stinging eyes. "I'll give you anything," he choked.

"Anything?" The black angel beat his wings, swirling the smoke around him in dark, suffocating eddies.

Withers breath caught. And then he said, "Anything. Everything!"

Morgenstern laughed in his face. Withers felt the ropes loosen and fall away. He staggered up from the chair and the room pitched as he swooned from the sudden pain in his head. The beast caught him and held him up.

Withers cried out as Morgenstern's hand plunged into his abdomen. The dark man pushed his flesh aside and slid his hands up under Withers' ribs. The thinning air in the room was overtaken by thickening smoke. He was suffocating. His vision dimmed. His hearing lessened. From far away he heard a voice that said, "Never repent."

Withers felt a ripping in his body that eclipsed every other sensation of pain he'd experienced, in war, on the force, in sickness. Every hard thing in his life was a joy compared to what Morgenstern did with his hand. And as much as he wanted to black out, to fall out of the world into blissful oblivion, he was held right there, in his body, feeling every searing tug and jerk and tear. Until Morgenstern pulled his hand free and held it up, showing Withers a wetly shining mass of meat — the meat that had once been killing Withers.

The magician tore at it with white teeth until a piece the size of a plum came off and the thing swallowed it like a pelican eating a fish: chin up, tissue sliding down.

"Want a taste?" he asked.

Withers squinted his eyes shut as hard as he could and shook his head like a child being offered ipecac.

"You don't know what you're missing. None of you have any taste, really." Two more bites and the ball of rebellious flesh was gone. Morgenstern picked Withers up in his arms and carried him outside the trailer. He set the man down in the grass by the fence. People rushed around them with buckets and hoses trying to put out the fire. None of them paid the men any mind.

"What did you just do? Did I just sell you my soul?"

Morgenstern laughed again. "Of all the things you have — this planet, your time on it, a comfortable life in a universe hostile to *everything*… and still, you want a soul. Don't be so greedy. You already got more than you deserve."

The magician left to get a bucket to help put out the fire. Withers heard him shout, "My God, Lili's in there!" as though he meant it.

Withers rolled over in the grass and pushed himself up off the ground. He took a deep breath in the night air and relished it.

One Last Drop Of Blood To Remember Me By
Matt Moore

I don't want to go down these stairs and see that face reflected back at me. The one I haven't seen in decades.

"Come on, Jackie!" Annabelle yells from somewhere in the cottage. "Don't want to be late."

Sunlight slants in the western-facing windows painting golden rectangles on the floor planks beneath me, the steps leading down, the small foyer below. Annabelle's bag is already down there next to the mirror. The mirror, she said, to remind people what's past and appreciate what's to come. To understand the gifts this decades-old cottage she calls "Bimini" can bestow.

Annabelle has no idea what this weekend has meant to me. Not just being free of glass grinding in my knuckles when I grab something or having clear vision instead of everything looking all blurry on the right. Here, it's like I never wasted the last forty years. Healthy years sublimating career goals into being the good wife or finding excuses when mother nagged about children. Long, lonely years wondering why I couldn't truly love Trevor.

Here, I could start again and not lie to myself.

And I can't keep lying to Annabelle.

So I grab my suitcase, effortlessly, then I'm down the stairs, watching my shoes appear in the mirror. My tan slacks follow, then a sensible blouse, and finally the impossibly young face of a woman who won't learn she's dying for decades.

There's footsteps behind me and I turn as she emerges from the cellar door, her jet-black hair without a strand of silver. But she still radiates that self-assuredness she possessed when we met. That poise that made something within me stir, and then a pang of confusion and guilt.

Annabelle asks, "So. Ready?"

I set my suitcase down. "I'm not leaving."

* * *

I stay down in the basement because I know Jackie needs a little more time to get ready to leave. A chill washes over me that she's stalling like others have to try to get us to spend another night. Like those others, she's gone quiet, changing ages suddenly over the course of the weekend. I never should have brought up those scars on her forearms. Barely noticeable at her true age, they became pale ridges in her skin whenever she fell into her teens. When I mentioned them, she grabbed at her arms and told me they were nothing.

But what's done is done and if there's more than I thought going on behind her blue eyes, I can't let her think she has a choice in leaving.

With the power and water turned off, I padlock the fuse box shut and hook the chain through the pump handle to secure it in the off position. I call out: "Come on, Jackie! Don't want to be late."

Above me, the stairs creak in that familiar pattern of someone descending. I go up the cellar stairs, young legs pumping, and emerge at the door between the foyer and the kitchen. Jackie stands before the mirror, as I knew she would, suitcase in hand and somewhere in her mid-twenties. She turns and her age flickers—spots appearing and fading, weight gaining and melting from her hips. Just like my sister the day she died.

I dig my nails into my palm to keep from being pulled into those memories. Focusing on Jackie, I put on my *I'm-in-charge* smile and say, "So. Ready?" I shut the thick wooden cellar door.

Instead of admitting that she is, she sets down her suitcase and tells me, "I'm not leaving." She drifts up to her actual age, flowing red hair turning white, her skin pale as a cloudy winter day. But those eyes, which caught my attention the day she moved into the residence, remain brilliant blue. Except now they're shot with red veins caused by, I hope, gathering tears.

I move to her and take her by the shoulders. She's trembling. "Jackie, we talked about this, remember?" I say. "I told you that you wouldn't want to leave and made you promise that you would. Are you breaking your promise to me?"

"You didn't tell me..." she stammers, her age still flickering. Crow's feet carve into the skin around her eyes, then smooth into nothing. "You said it would be *like* we were young—"

"You wouldn't believe me if I told you, would you? Now we have to go, but we can come back next weekend." It's a lie. It will take months of long conversations before I think about letting Jackie come back.

"I'm dying, Annabelle," she says. "Cancer."

The word snatches my breath away.

"In my brain," Jackie continues. "The clumsiness. Trembling. Not arthritis. Blurred vision isn't cataracts. Doctors say it's too late to operate. If they'd caught it two or three years ago, maybe. I have perhaps one good year left. Didn't want to tell you. Afraid you wouldn't... with me, want to..."

"Oh, Jackie." I try to embrace her, but she pushes me away like I'm some stranger.

"But Trevor's retirement savings. I could hire a surgeon. Rent equipment. Bring them here. I become a few years younger. When the tumor was operable."

My heart turns to ice. "Don't fall into that trap. There's nothing here. It's a pause, not an escape. Your life is out there—"

"My *death* is out there!" Her breath comes in hitches and gulps.

Her words break my heart, but I've had it broken before and, like everything, it will heal. "Then let's make the most of the time you have left." I wait for her reply and, when I don't get one, try to kiss her, but she pulls away. She loses forty years in an instant, then snaps back to her true age.

I have to get us moving again. My certainty has convinced others that staying here is not an option, so I grab my bag and the cooler with the leftover food, and head out the door. Across the porch and down the flagstone walk to the crushed-shell driveway, I wait for but don't hear Jackie behind me. A cool late-afternoon breeze carries the scent of the sea, rattling the underbrush that surrounds Bimini and hides it from the small bay beyond. I load the things into the trunk of my car and when I return inside she's gone. My heart stops and I choke back a sob. I check the bathroom, then head upstairs to the bedrooms, calling her name. Not finding her, I go down to the basement, wondering if she's locked herself in the storage room. Returning to the main level, the tang of sea air guides me into the kitchen to find the sliding back door open a few inches. I throw it open and step onto the deck. Not seeing her, I scream: "Jackie!"

* * *

She tries to kiss me. Maybe she wants to soothe me, but I don't want to be soothed. I duck her, just like Monica What's-Her-Name at Trevor's office party, both of us drunk. I'd egged her on, wanting to embarrass Trevor. Then I couldn't go through with it and hated myself for months for thinking of it.

Annabelle grabs her bag and cooler, and goes outside.

Maybe I should follow and apologize before I ruin everything.

When we'd met, I admired Annabelle's confidence, her toned legs, the flattering fit of her jacket. She looked to only be in her fifties. Someone said she'd been a history teacher in private schools. She even wrote a few books. So why did she live at a residence full of the old, the sick, the dying? They start us in full apartments, then winnow us to assisted studios, single bedrooms, the rooms we'll die in. Our future locked away in a windowless hallway, one end blocked, a crowd pressing behind you, impossible to turn back.

She was the one who approached me, inviting me for tea, but it became something more. I resisted, at first, and when I couldn't deny it, I insisted we be discreet.

Now, I need to take charge. For once in my life.

While I still have it.

I rush into the kitchen. Bacon and coffee smells still linger in the air. We'd been so playful making breakfast. Finally, a real couple. I grab a kitchen knife from a drawer, unlock the back door, slide it open, and step onto the back porch.

A day ago, she led me out this door and down a twisting narrow path. We became teenagers and lounged on a small beach on a tiny, secluded bay. I saw a whole new life in front of me, one where I wouldn't hate myself.

We giggled about the other women in the residence the way girls giggle over boys. Who was cute? How far we would go.

I should have told her, but would it have made a difference? Something nagging at me all weekend becomes clear. Her confidence, that calm determination. She believes she's always right. I felt drawn to it because I needed her to make decisions, just like mother and Trevor did for me. But now fear coils deep within me. Because she'll never share Bimini. Not completely. If I lived twenty more years, this would never be *our* place.

Hers. Always.

At the edge of the underbrush, an axe, rusty with age, leans against the woodpile.

Too bulky.

I sprint behind the cottage to the corner, joints pain-free. Leaning against the grey cedar shingles, I peer around. No sign of Annabelle near the car. Because she's inside, calling my name. I dash to the car, kneel down on the far side and jab the knife at the tire. Muscles flex, sweat gathering in my armpits. It's euphoric. Dry air whooshes out, the rear end settling.

Footsteps on the deck. "Jackie!" Annabelle cries. Some instinct drives me into the bramble. Branches slap my face, grab at my clothing. I crouch behind a thick bush. Annabelle comes around the corner, shading her eyes with a hand. "Come on, this is crazy."

I wipe at something on my face and my fingertips come away bloody.

"The electricity and water are off and locked shut." She drifts the other way, going around back. "Maybe you think you can pry open the locks and get things turned on, but there's no food here and it's a six-mile walk to town."

But there are neighbors. There were turn-offs along the twisting route in. They could get me to town where

I'd arrange transportation back to the city. I take out my phone, hoping to pull up a map, but there's no signal, just as Annabelle had said when telling me not to bring it. *I don't want to have to compete with those games of yours,* she told me. Now I understand the real reason.

But if I can find a signal, call for help. Then record directions. I won't need Annabelle to come back.

But if she gets in my way?

I activate the phone's camera.

The ocean-blown wind carries Annabelle's voice. "Jackie, when I get the tire fixed, I will leave you here. Come on out and let's talk."

I believe her. Because I know why I ran. I'm afraid. The nagging suspicion about her being selfish? There's more to it.

It's a voice from the ground. A young woman.

Her name's Corinne. Annabelle's sister.

And Annabelle murdered her to gain possession of Bimini.

* * *

Flattening only one tire gives me hope that she's not completely gone. Others just ran off into the underbrush, but Jackie wants to keep me here. To talk, I hope, but I'm ready if she comes at me with whatever she used on the tire.

"Jackie, when I get the tire fixed, I will leave you here," I call out, hoping the threat will get some response. Getting none, I circle the house, calling to her and straining to see into the gathering gloom in the thick bramble.

I'd hoped my time with Jackie would be like the seven wonderful years with Marie. Or the quick, intense eighteen months with Gwen. Time spent here, playing like we're young again, but having friends and activities back in the city we couldn't wait to return to so Bimini would never get too strong a hold on us.

A widow of two years, Jackie told me she moved into the residence to escape the memories of her husband in her home. She shared stories I'd heard before about a marriage that never quite worked. A woman who blamed herself for its failing and would let those burdens drive her into the grave. A woman who didn't see her future, who I couldn't help but fall for so I could show her one. We kept things quiet as Jackie became comfortable loving another woman and so told no one about coming here.

I arrive back at the porch and having seen no sign of her I move back inside, lock the porch door, grab Jackie's bags on my way out the front, and lock it. In the driveway, I take my bags out of the trunk, get out the jack and the spare, and then pop off the hub cap. I remove my jacket despite the offshore breeze as evening creeps in. I'll go slow, hoping Jackie will come to me.

I really didn't think Jackie would be like those six women and one man who disappeared into the shrub-oak and bayberry. All these decades later, I've never found a trace—no clothes, bones, jewelry. Gone, like their regret swallowed them completely and pulled them back into those long-gone moments. Like their older selves who'd arrived at the cottage never came to be. Most of those I've brought here—friends, lovers and those in-between—appreciated the gift Bimini gave and the clarity it brought: that youth is the absence of both regret and wisdom. But the regrets carried by those seven overwhelmed any desire they had to enjoy however much life they had left. That first time I waited three days before giving up. But since then I've waited less and put preparations in place.

I smash my fist into the crushed-shell driveway, drawing blood but yanking my attention away from the all-consuming past.

"You'd leave me here?" a teen girl's quaking voice yells from the underbrush.

"I don't want to," I reply over my shoulder. I brush sand and shell from my bloody knuckles, finding the wounds already healed. I get to work on the first lug nut. "But if you won't come out, I won't stay."

Branches snap. I stand, facing the sound and movement that resolves into a gangly teenaged girl in women's clothes, like she's playing dress-up, moving out of the underbrush. She holds a kitchen knife in her right hand. Scratches crisscross her face. Her scleras have gone pink.

"Put the knife down, Jackie, and let's talk about what happens now."

"Will you help me find a surgeon?" she asks, shifting her feet, shell pieces crunching. Blood weeps from the scratches, running down her face to gather at her chin. "Get equipment? Let me come back?"

"No," I tell her, hoping the certainty in my voice will end this.

Instead, the knife point flicks up.

"Jackie, honey," I continue, "it's not just the surgery. Think about the recovery time, the chemo and radiation. The pain. And there's no way to know that the tumor won't be there as soon as you leave."

Blood drips from her chin to the white shells pieces. "I'll take that chance."

"And what if the surgery doesn't work? You could die—"

"I'm dying now!"

"We all have to die." The lie is sour on my lips.

"Is that what you told Corinne?"

157

I fight to not react. Only two others have heard Corinne so soon after coming here and neither of them ever left, but I won't dwell on that.

"She's lying, Jackie," I say. "When Corinne died—"

"When you killed her."

"Jackie—"

The blade flicks to the cooler. "I'm taking that. And the keys to the cottage. If you try to stop me, I'll tell everyone about this place."

I've lived with this threat my whole life and my father before that. The defense is: who would believe it? It takes time to hear the voices coming up from the ground. Few of the workers who hooked up electricity or built the rooms in the basement noticed anything wrong except that the cottage was unusually remote and every day there seemed to be a twist in the road they didn't remember. The ones who have, young men with downcast eyes who never smiled, said they felt uneasy but couldn't say why.

"No one will believe you. They'll say the tumor—"

She takes her iPhone, which I told her not to bring, from a pants pocket. "They'd believe the video. Me changing ages."

I drop down, grab the tire iron, and come back up before Jackie can react.

"Don't," she says, knife pointed at me.

But I do, swinging the heavy tool. I can't let her have that kind of leverage over me. Jackie twists away, pulling the phone out of range but the knife comes up. I dodge away instinctively, but my feet get tangled and I fall.

Jackie flickers through ages, losing and gaining decades in the blink of an eye. "I just want to live!" she screams, syllables ricocheting from sweet-little-girl soprano to husky sixty-three-year-old alto.

"But there's no life here. There's nothing here. Honey, I know what Corinne is saying, but I didn't kill her to have this place just for me."

Jackie moves at me, but I bring the tire iron up, getting to my feet. Jackie reconsiders. "Go ahead. Leave me!" She drops into her twenties and runs back into the bramble.

I wait until the sounds of her moving through the underbrush fade. I sit down hard, shells pinching through my slacks, tears welling up. I move my fingers over where Jackie's blood fell. There's no trace of it, but a few shoots of grass push up through the shells.

I resume work on the tire, understanding that the video was an empty threat and she's gone. Soon her voice will join the others.

As children, our father told Corinne and me not to listen. I don't know if Corinne obeyed or not, but it was my one rebellion. The stories told by those whose blood has been spilled here in languages I didn't know but could understand — French, Aboriginal, Viking, Spanish, and more — fascinated me. Centuries of murder, revenge, disease, and starvation on this rocky and remote point where my father had Bimini built. They awakened an interest in history, wanting to learn about this place. How all those moments added up to this very moment.

Now Corinne overpowers them all, but Jackie's blood is so fresh that I can make out some whisperings against the cacophony I have learned to ignore. All Jackie sees is the surgery, but I pause in mid-turn when I realize that she's going to try to reach the shore, or wait until I've left and head for town on foot. If she can find a cell signal, she'll call for help and upload the video to the Web. She'll post it everywhere if I don't help, drawing people with regrets eating at them, then scientists who'll rip the ground apart for whatever ancient secret lies dreaming here. Everything I've fought for, killed for, will be ruined.

Things used to be much simpler, but that is the past.

I could leave her here, assuming that when she got too far from Bimini, her symptoms would return and force her to turn back. But she's determined. I have to try to find her, take her in my arms, and help her make peace with her fate. If not, maybe she'll follow me into the basement.

I stand, put my jacket on against the cooling air, and move into the underbrush.

"Jackie, come back!" I yell. "We can stay here another night if you'll just come back. But let me explain about Corinne!"

* * *

Corinne's terrified screams are everywhere. Annabelle drove a wedge between her and their father. He disowned Corinne and gave everything to Annabelle. And when Annabelle caught Corinne here, Annabelle killed her.

And she'll kill me. This cottage. It's so remote and no one knows I'm here.

Every few steps, the salt-tinged wind shifts. I can't find that path to the shore. Inky shadows getting longer and every tree and bush looks like every other one.

"Jackie, come back!" The wind almost carries her voice away. "We can stay here another night if you'll just come back. But let me explain about Corinne! Our father was very strict, but she was a rebel. She didn't help at the store and dated older men without my father's permission. Sometimes she disappeared for weeks."

Something tickles down my right arm. I scratch at it and keep moving.

Annabelle says, "I was the good daughter. Afraid my father would discover I wasn't interested in marrying some young man who could take over the business. I never misbehaved.

"When Corinne was twenty and I was seventeen, she'd been gone for six weeks when we got a letter from her saying she was in San Francisco and had gotten married. My father was furious and he changed the will, cutting her off from everything. He left Bimini to me."

The tickle is now an itch. Looking down, there's three parallel cuts across my forearm like ladder rungs. I'm drawing the blade across my skin, slicing a fourth. Instead of pain, ecstasy. Like being fifteen, up in my room where mother said I should be. Not at student council debates. Not out with friends. Blood is revenge. Scars making her perfect daughter imperfect.

My blood drips from my fingertips. I long to spill Annabelle's.

"Two years later, we found Corinne here. My father was so angry and told her to leave, but I begged him to let me talk to her. She kept changing ages as she told me about her marriage falling apart."

I draw the blade from ribs to navel, edge biting deep. Pain I control, pain I decide. Bright and beautiful, rendering mother's guilt and Trevor's accusations to feeble nattering.

Movement to my left. I turn and catch a glimpse of her struggling through the bramble. If I can get the keys, I won't need my phone.

I clutch the knife tighter.

Annabelle says, "She wanted to start again and undo all the bad decisions she'd made. I told her we can't change the past. But I said if she got help and got her life back on track, our father might change his mind and take her back."

I move behind a fallen tree, thick stump half my height, and peer through the delta of stump, ground, and trunk. Come closer, Annabelle.

"That night, she woke me up and told me she'd found a voice I needed to hear. I followed her out into the brush where she hit me with a rock. She accused me of convincing our father to give me Bimini. She said she needed it. Couldn't leave it. I didn't mean to hurt her, Jackie, but it wasn't her anymore. Like all her regrets had overpowered the sister I knew."

I grab a fist-sized stone and call out, "Annabelle, I've caught my leg. I'm stuck. Help me!" She moves toward me. Steps away and she still hasn't seen me. I toss the stone to her left. She turns. I spring, swinging hard. The knife cuts air. Looking down, I lock eyes with a five-year-old girl, lost in adult clothing. Instinct to not harm children freezes me.

Youth-quick, she snatches a handful of sand. Flings it in my face.

My hands come up. Not fast enough.

I swing blindly and hit something solid. Meaty. A scream. The knife yanks from my grip. Blinking away grit, I make out Annabelle running and struggling out of her jacket, the blade caught in folds of fabric. Or deeper. Wipe a hand across my eyes and my vision clears. She's gone. I find her jacket a few paces on. Blood stains it from armpit to fringe. Several steps more. The knife, slick with blood. I snatch it up to reveal green grass beneath, the side touching the ground pristine.

Sprinting, I break from the tree line as Annabelle rounds the corner toward the front door. I pursue. Seconds later, moving with such speed, I leap up the porch steps. Drops of blood lead across the pale wooden planks to the open front door. I follow. Just a glimpse in the mirror reveals a twisted, bloody thing, eyes just scarlet orbs.

Blood leads to the cellar door and I race down. Hot water heater and water pump locked shut. Blood splatter on the concrete floor twists right. Down a hallway. Walls primer-white. Two doors to the left, but the blood leads to a third one at the end. I run to it, heart thudding. Door's new. Not like the ancient wooden doors upstairs. Shove the door open, tumble in, slashing.

Not here.

Room is ten feet square. Cardboard boxes stacked on old furniture. Light from a small window high on the rear wall. No other doors. No place to go.

Where are you hiding, Annabelle?

My breath coming in gasps. Blood flows over my lips.

Grab a box. Yank it. Comes away too easily. Empty.

Kick another. Bounces away. Empty —

Door clicks behind me. I spin. A pneumatic arm installed above it. Chrome glistening, plastic bright. It's pulled the door shut. No handle on this side.

Trapped.

This whole room. A trap.

"Where are you!" Bloody spittle flies. Must find her. Her blood will save me. Cure me.

"Jackie!" Her voice. Upstairs or outside. "Please listen. This place feeds on your regrets and suffering. It wants your blood. Please think about what you're doing. It's not too late. I want to help you!"

The window. Too small.

But not for a child. The chair positioned beneath it. Bloody fingerprints on the pane.

Clever, Annabelle.

Up on the chair. Yank the sash open. Cool air across my face. Salt-tinged. Shadows gathered across the lawn.

Boost myself up and recall lying to mother that I wasn't invited to Jill's sleepover. Easier to avoid the fight. The window balloons from impossibly small to a tight fit. I crawl forward, elbows on the sill. Clothes voluminous, hard to move in. Head is out, then the arm with the knife.

I prop an elbow against the foundation. A shadow moves.

*   *   *

I hope she won't figure out the window. Three of the four I led down there did, emerging as bloody, horrid things. But the fourth, beautiful and broken Alicia, gave up, finally listening to me and realizing she needed to get away. A month later, after so many tears, Alicia wasted her life and threw herself from her twelfth-floor balcony.

But the window slides open and the back of her head emerges, tiny in its youth and red hair lustrous. Then a skinny arm lost in a too-big blouse unfolds out, a knife in its bony fist. The elbow braces against the foundation and more of her slides out.

I move forward, my long shadow falling over her and I raise up the axe, the motion pulling apart the already healing wound in my side, sending a fresh trickle of blood down my leg. I ignore it and swing to finish this in one, merciful blow. The axe lands true with a sickening crack, flattening the skull. Bright, rich blood flows up and around the axe, pooling around the convulsing body's crushed head. I yank the axe free, spraying blood and grey bits of brain, then drop the axe and grab the twitching arms before gravity pulls the body back through the window. I drag the tiny body into the underbrush, leaving a smear of blood in the sand and beach grass. Its clothing bunches up and catches in the weeds and bramble, revealing the cuts in her arm. I push down pity since there's nothing I can do. A dozen steps into the brush I drop her, knowing that the next time I return there will be no trace. Thankfully, the body has finally gone still, its death throes over. The wound in my side throbs.

I dig in the pockets of her blood-soaked clothing until I find her phone, which I take. If only she'd listened to me, but if she didn't, then I doubt she ever would, so this is for the best.

Heading back, the sky as grey as Bimini's shingles, I find the ground has soaked up most of the blood, drawing it down into itself. In another minute or so, there will be no trace just as there is none of mine. And already the brown grass has gone green, fresh blades emerging from the sandy soil. Flowers bloom on what had been bare bushes.

And with her blood, this place absorbs all the life she had yet to live that she shed to take the younger form. Life that this place will grant me, her killer, like some kind of reward or tribute, just as it did with Corinne.

When we fought, Corinne changed to a toddler, when she had short hair, because I'd grabbed a handful of her long, flowing hair. But I'd given a hard enough tug that she stumbled, fell and — fighting for my life — I struck her in the face with a rock. Then I ran back to my father, sobbing, and told him she had attacked me. When I showed him where she had hit me behind my ear, the wound had already healed. He demanded to know where Corinne was, thinking the blood in my hair was hers, but I panicked and said I didn't know. But already her voice was coming up from the ground. He searched for her corpse, but did not find her.

The next morning, my father banished me from Bimini, separating me from the voices whose stories I wanted to tell. In the city, I found my bank accounts closed.

So I wandered, trying to make a life as a single, unmarried woman. In the 1920s, it was a challenge and sometimes I had to rely on a man to support me. Still, I worked and studied, earning a PhD and teaching at private girls schools. All the while, I refused to feel guilt or regret for what I'd had to do. History cannot be changed. Learn its lessons, but what's done is done.

My father shunned me for decades as I gracefully grew older. People mistook me for being younger, sometimes by over a decade, and I came to understand the power of Corinne's death.

Eventually, my father asked me to come home. I found him at Bimini flickering between ages, in the grips of dementia. He wailed how he had failed to protect his daughters, protect this place. So I waited and watched, learned the youngest age he would return to and, when it was merciful, ended his suffering.

With concentration, you can hear past Corinne and listen to my father along with the other friends and lovers I have had to kill here. Some in self-defense, like Jackie, and others so near the end that most of them willingly gave up their lives so I could live longer. Be a witness to history.

Most of them.

And their voices join the others whose blood has been spilled here. Which is how you can hear mine, whoever you are. Perhaps you're a squatter, having broken into this place during the long and dark winter months, and wondered what has bothered you like a voice you can't quite make out. Maybe you're a trusted friend, a new lover, or my wife, hearing my voice from years ago after I've taught you how to change ages. Or perhaps you have bought this property after my unlikely death and have learned this place's secrets.

The wound in my side is nearly healed so here's one last drop of blood so you'll understand I'm not a monster. The future is not a windowless hall closed at the end, as Jackie saw it, but a wondrous, endless one where I walk with some for a time, let them go, and walk with others. This is a more complex age, true, but one where a new identity can be purchased, or a bored and tired civil servant can be convinced to change the date on my driver license because of course I'm not seventy-seven, but fifty-seven.

I'll return inside, change my bloodied and torn blouse, destroy Jackie's phone, and clean up the house like I have so many times before. In the morning, I'll change the tire, find a place to dump Jackie's things, and return to the residence. I'll pretend to worry and agree when someone finally wonders if poor Jackie might have harmed herself.

In the meantime, there's a new woman there who wears the burdens of a long, regretful life on her face. Perhaps she'd like to go for tea.

Fly Away Home
Elizabeth Massie

Angie perched on a straight-back chair beside the window, leaning over her knees, smiling at Molly. But the smile was not pleasant. It had been once, long ago, a smile full of gaiety and innocence, but now it was fearsome. Her lips were a darker red than was natural, and her teeth were sharp and much too white. The skin of her face was taut and hugged the bone as if it had been steamed on. Her eyes were a deep, pure black, and reflected none of the light of the room.

Molly glanced at Angie, shivered violently, and then looked back at her sewing machine. "I've given up my dream of flying," she said as she rethreaded the needle then pumped the treadle, forcing the fabric through. "I've other dreams now, and they have nothing to do with taking off into the sky. I'm a woman now, not a fanciful child. And women don't fly. Now, go away. I told you to never bother me again, yet here you are."

Angie leaned farther down so Molly could see her face. She continued to smile. She was petite and trim, with red, curly hair she'd never been able to tame quite right, and she'd once been cute, charming. But now...no, not now. Not anymore.

"I told you that you could not be shed of me," Angie said. "And I am here with a gift. Even after all this time, after the way you've treated me, I am here to make your dream come true. You've always wanted to fly. Oh, how I heard that enough from you. Over and over again! Now I will make the impossible possible. Can't you appreciate that?"

Molly shook her head. "You're being foolish. You have no plane and you have no money. Get away, Angie. I haven't time for your childish prattle."

But Angie just grinned her sharp-toothed grin and re-crossed her ankles beneath her long, gray skirt. She held out a packet of cigarettes. "Want one?"

"You know I can't. It would get me in trouble. Now leave."

Angie tipped her head and her hell-dark eyes narrowed. "You still hate me, don't you?"

"I...I don't hate you. I've never hated you. You were always my friend."

Angie laughed, a shrill and painful sound. "Liar! I do wonder about that, Molly. Yet in spite of your hatred, here I am, bringing you a wonderful gift!" Angie lit a cigarette and blew a tendril of smoke in Molly's direction. Then she laughed again, kicked up out of the chair, and left.

Thank God, thank God, Molly thought. Her heart hammered. She leaned over her machine and closed her eyes to calm herself, to shake the image of Angie from her mind, and then went back to her task. She needed to finish this blouse and the other blouses in her basket before 6 p.m., when the factory closed. If she didn't, a foreman would make note and dock her pay. As the only working member of her family, that was the last thing she would allow happen. Molly saw herself as one of the factory's best employees, though her work was tedious and caused her back and arms to ache. She always took a shorter lunch break than her co-workers did. She never broke the rules, such as other girls did when they sneaked buttons and thread home or smoked forbidden cigarettes by holding them low beneath their machines then exhaling into their collars.

Curse Angie and her intrusion! Molly wished she had never known her.

As Molly steered the bleached cotton beneath the needle, watching carefully in case it decided to snag or catch, she thought back on the days when, yes, her biggest desire was to fly. Back on the salty, sandy shores of North Carolina's Outer Banks where she, her father, mother, and brothers had a small cottage on the narrow strip of land between the Currituck Sound and the Atlantic Ocean.

Her father, Frank, had been a Kitty Hawk fisherman, taking his boat out for days at a time and coming home smelling of brine, flounder, and satisfaction. Her older brother, Ralph, was a surfman with the Kitty Hawk Life Saving Station. Her younger brother Simon was simple-minded, and spent his time digging holes in the sandy soil and chasing ghost crabs. Molly loved everything about the sand and the salt, the wind-twisted shrubs, the way herring gulls and terns hovered in the slate-gray skies and pelicans flew steady lines along the horizon. Her best friend was Angie, a fun-filled, freckle-faced girl who could always make Molly laugh. The girls didn't attend school, but taught themselves to read and write using newspapers and the Sears, Roebuck and Company catalog that came in the mail to Molly's mother, Judith. The girls took music lessons from Mrs. Taylor, a widow who was as grizzled and sandblasted as a fisherman's shack and yet, in her little parlor, had a fine piano.

It was in September, the year Molly and Angie turned thirteen, that true excitement came to the Outer Banks by way of two brothers from Ohio. They set up tents south of Kitty Hawk at the dunes of Kill Devil Hills, and spent their time building and experimenting with gliders large and strong enough to carry a man. Handsome, the both of them, and strong, with faces locked in determination and bright with intelligence.

Molly immediately fell in love with the younger of the two, Orville. Though he was quite a bit older, it did not stop her from thinking of him as she fished for crabs or waded in the surf. It did not stop her from riding her bicycle, her prized possession, to visit them at their camp to watch them measure and tinker, hammer and bolt and argue, and then test their inventions in the powerful, steady sea winds.

Orville, with his charming mustache and bright eyes, noticed Molly one afternoon, and teased her, asking if she thought men would fly someday. Molly replied, "Oh, of course!" Then he asked if she thought ladies would fly someday, too. She said, "Oh, of course, for I've seen the wind buffet men and women equally, knocking us all to our faces without care for our sex. So shouldn't it lift us equally, as well?" This made Orville chuckle with appreciation.

Angie, who traveled with Molly wherever she went, whispered, "Why are you making eyes at that man? He is not much younger than your father!"

Molly said, "Hush, Angie. It's my business."

Orville and his brother Wilbur left for Ohio when the weather grew cold and came back again the following summer. They continued modifying and testing their gliders from the tall dunes of Kill Devil Hills. Molly watched as time and time again they took turns climbing onto the glider and taking off with the wind, jumping up and down, ecstatic at each successful attempt as Angie stood with arms crossed.

Yet the brothers had plans beyond gliders. They were determined to build a flying machine, one that did not depend on wind to keep it aloft. They returned to Ohio yet again, leaving Molly melancholy and short-tempered. She found herself arguing with Angie and slapping her simple-minded brother when he got in her way. She lost her appetite and shed ten pounds in three weeks. She wrote letters to Orville, filled with passion and heartache, then tore them up and threw them into the brine. Her mother didn't know what to do with her, but to leave her alone.

"Molly," Angie would complain. "Don't treat me so! We are friends 'til the end, aren't we?"

And Molly would apologize, hug Angie, and say, "Yes, forever."

In the fall of 1903, the brothers returned to Kill Devil Hills once more. This time they were ready to try out the flying machine they'd built and shipped from Ohio. After more alterations and several failed attempts, they prepared to test again on the morning of December 17th.

The Wright brothers' local assistants and other curious men gathered around the wind-blown dunes, wrapped in their wool jackets and caps. Molly and Angie, now shapely girls of sixteen, stood back a bit, scarves around their necks, holding hands, waiting.

Waiting, hearts pounding.

As Orville climbed onto the machine and Wilbur steadied the wings to launch it from the metal tracks, Molly said, "Oh, I hope my dear Orville is successful! And one day, I shall fly, too!"

Angie leaned close to be heard over the wind, and whined, "Do you love Orville more than me, Molly?"

"Shh, be quiet," Molly insisted.

"Molly, answer me."

"Hush, now! Let's watch and not talk!"

Angie's hand was instantly, painfully cold in Molly's own, so frosty-sharp that Molly jerked hers away and turned, wide-eyed, to stare at her friend.

But Angie was gone. Molly squinted, turned about, shaded her eyes, but couldn't catch a glimpse of Angie running off.

What's the matter with her, anyway? So jealous of my affections! How selfish!

There was a loud rattling, and the great flying machine was traveling along the rails and then it was aloft, rising slightly but certainly, traveling under its own power. John Daniels, one of the few men in Kitty Hawk who owned a camera, snapped a photo. It felt as if everything within viewing distance held its breath in that moment — gulls overhead went silent, the wind softened, and even the crashing waves along the shore below seemed to go still. The plane skimmed the air then landed 120 feet away. The men cheered. Molly jumped and clapped, feeling as if she, herself, were up there as well. More attempts followed, with Wilbur manning the last trial of the day and flying a full 852 feet.

When the sun set over the pewter waters of the sound and the local gawkers had scattered from the dunes, the two brothers and their helpers, giddy with the thrill of success, went into Kitty Hawk to celebrate at the *White Fin*. Molly joined the men, the most daring thing she had ever done, for the *White Fin* was a man's place, a poorly-lit, gritty-floored, splinter-walled shack where fishermen and surfmen gathered to drink, curse, and fight. She found a small, empty table near the rear door, and was surprised to see Angie standing in the deep shadows of the corner.

"Where have you been?" Molly asked as Angie slid onto the bench next to her.

"It doesn't matter. I'm here now."

Molly nodded and put her arm around her friend to draw her close in a hug. But then she flinched and let go. Angie looked different. Her freckles seemed to have bled across her face in irregular patches. Her blue eyes were smaller, darker, sharper, reminding Molly of a lizard's eyes.

"Angie…" Molly gasped.

"What, Molly? You are my friend." Angie tilted her head, looking severe and cruel in the faint light. "Is something wrong?"

Molly turned away quickly to watch as Mrs. Richardson, the old woman who owned the bar, brought her the beer she had ordered. Then, cautiously, she turned back to Angie, who now appeared as sweet and cute as she always had.

Dear me! I'm more tired than I realized. My fatigue is playing terrible tricks on my eyes.

Angie ordered a beer, and the two girls gingerly sipped (Molly, having never had beer before, found it to be quite foul, though Angie thought hers was dandy) and watched the men. Molly knew them all — friends and acquaintances of her father and her brother. For this reason she had no fear any would attempt to offend or molest them. However, a few gave her stern looks, for they clearly wondered if Judith knew where her daughter was.

The men sat at tables and booths, downing their beers and toasting each other and the brilliant work of the brothers from Ohio. Wilbur, clearly in his cups, leaned on the bar, recounting his conquering of the air to Mrs. Richardson's meek husband, whose job it was to draw beer from the keg and serve crab fritters. Orville sat with one elbow on his table, listening to one of the men recount the flights with inebriated glee. Every so often, he glanced in Molly's direction and smiled.

It was those smiles that made the nasty beer, the dank darkness of the bar, and the stink of the place tolerable. Molly shyly returned the smiles, and made a plan to speak to him before she went home.

She didn't realize until her mug was empty that Angie had, once more, vanished without a sound.

Nearing midnight, Orville, a bit tottery, left the bar and went outside. Molly placed her coins on the table and quickly followed, catching Orville on the street in the pale, misted light from the window of the Kitty Hawk Mercantile.

She called, "Mr. Wright? Would you please take me for a ride on your machine before you leave? I want to fly!"

He turned to her, smiled again, and said, "It's only built for one."

"I weigh very little."

Orville scratched his chin. "You are such a pretty young lady. So different from several years ago. You were a child then, I remember."

Molly nodded.

"But still not yet a woman."

"I'm sixteen since May."

Orville stepped close and took her arm. He pulled her to him and she closed her eyes, preparing for him to kiss her fully on her lips. But he pecked her lightly on the cheek, instead, and then let her go.

"Write me in Ohio when you are a woman," he said. "And I shall come and take you for a ride in the clouds. By then, my brother and I will have perfected our machine and we will be able to travel for miles at a time, I have no doubt!"

Then he was gone, moving into a roiling fog that had traveled into town on the cold sea air.

What age will that be? she wondered as she put her hands into her skirt pockets. *Another year? Two? Three?*

"No years," came a voice from the porch of the mercantile. It was Angie, leaning against the wall, staring hard. She was little more than a silhouette in the fog.

"You will never fly with the man. Forget about Orville, Molly. Forget about flying."

Molly said, "You don't know what you're talking about!"

"And you're full of *White Fin* beer. Let me walk you home."

Angie came off the porch and walked Molly home.

But Molly could not forget Orville. She wrote more letters, tore most of them up, but mailed a few of them. He wrote her back several times, but only postcards showing lovely Ohio countrysides. They were all versions of the same greeting — "Hello, Molly. I hope you are doing well. Best wishes, Orville."

"It doesn't matter that his cards are so impersonal," Molly told Angie as they sat on a damp blanket facing the ocean. It was early evening; the September sun was to their backs behind the town. Molly had just finished her day at the mercantile where she'd been employed for four months. Her shoes and stockings were off and her toes were dug deep in the cool sand. "As famous as he is, he can't write any suggestion of romance on a card. That might ruin him or cause rumors."

Angie sniffed and her jaw tightened. "If you insist on talking about Orville, I will leave again."

"But why, Angie? He promised to come soon and take me flying!"

"Enough, I said!"

"Are you jealous?"

"Molly!"

"Answer me! Are you jealous of Orville?"

Angie stood threw her arms out in disgust. Her hair came free of its pins and spun down around her face like a dense, curly veil. The sound she made was nearly a growl. Molly's stomach clenched at such a scene. "So you are jealous, then?"

"I thought you were my friend!" she said from behind her hair.

"Damn it. I am. You know that."

"I know nothing of the sort. Orville this, Orville that! Flying here! Flying there! I hate it!"

"Angie, stop talking like that! I will fly someday! I can think of nothing else as wonderful!"

"Be quiet! You hate me! You hate me!"

Molly jumped up and brushed back her friend's hair. And she screamed. Angie's face was a demon's face, eyes black with spots of red, curled lip and teeth as dreadful as those of a shark.

"Oh, my God!" screamed Molly, and she fell to the sand with her hands over her eyes. "What has happened to you? Go away! Go away!"

A moment later, she felt a hand on her shoulder and she recoiled. "Go away!"

"Molly." It was Ralph. Molly looked up, and began to sob.

Ralph kneeled beside his sister. "What's wrong, dear? I was coming to find you, and here you are on the beach, screaming."

"It was Angie! I don't know what's wrong with her! I don't know…"

But Ralph only shook his head and said, "Molly, listen to me. It's Father."

Molly swallowed, took a hitching breath; it cut. "What? What about Father?"

"Come with me."

Molly followed Ralph home, to find her mother wailing and her father lying on his bed, cold and still.

Now, without a father, the family could not manage. Ralph, who was engaged to marry a plain yet industrious Kitty Hawk girl, did what he could, but was also saving for his own household. And so Judith took Molly and

Simon north to New York to live with Judith's mother in
a crowded tenement building.

Angie came along.

Molly secured a job at a shirtwaist factory in the
Asch Building, and spent six days a week on the eighth
floor, hunched over the sewing machine in a stuffy room
with many other girls, mostly immigrants not long off
the ship. Sometimes Molly thought she could smell the
sea on the girls, the brine and the sun and the sand and it
was all she could do to keep from weeping. The factory
was far from the shore, pressed on all sides by stone and
beam and block and glass and pavement and steaming
pipes, steaming manure, steaming humanity.

Late at night, in the tiny room she shared with
Simon, she wrote to Orville. She tore up most of her
letters and mailed a scant few, reminding him that she
was a woman now and no longer a child. She was ready
for him to come take her away in his flying machine. She
wanted to fly; she needed to fly more than anything else
in her life. She needed to rise up, out, and away from the
life that now had her grounded in despair.

Angie visited some of those nights, uninvited but
relentless, coming in as silently as a cat as Simon slept,
sometimes appearing as sweet and hopeful as she did
back along the Outer Banks, but more often than not
bearing a frightening, devilish, and distorted visage of
anger and cold resentment. Molly learned to avert her
eyes when Angie appeared, never knowing what to
expect.

"Fool! Not another letter to Mr. Wright," Angie
snarled one evening as she appeared at the door then sat
on the foot of the bed Molly shared with her brother.
Molly shifted away, eyes downcast. Her breathing and
heart picked up painful rhythms. "Didn't you read the
newspaper this morning?" asked Angie. "Orville's

brother, Wilbur, was flying two days ago. He crashed and died."

"Yes, I saw," said Molly. "My heart grieves for Orville."

"You ignore me in favor of some ridiculous dream!" said Angie. Her breath was close now, and hot. "Do you see now how flying is wrong? Only birds are meant to fly."

"And butterflies," whispered Molly.

"You aren't a butterfly or a bird."

"I want to fly. It is my dream. You can't take it from me."

"Molly!" Angie grabbed Molly's shoulders. The mattress jostled, causing Simon to whimper in his sleep. Molly steeled herself then looked at her friend full on. Angie's face was pained and sad, sweet and harmless. Then in an instant it shifted to hateful, enraged, horrifying, demonic. Back then to harmless, then back again to terrifying. Her hands, which had let go of Molly's arm, were a girl's hands, then a monster's, then a girl's, the fingers changing rapidly from claws to fingers to claws. "Don't do this to me!"

The hammering of Molly's heart stole her courage but not her resolve.

"I'm...I'm doing nothing to you, Angie."

"Why do you hate me? Why do you want nothing to do with me?"

Say what you need to say, Molly. Have this done with once and for all!

"Angie," she whispered, looking at the floor, her throat dry with fear. "I can't bear this anymore. Listen to me, and listen well. You're a creature of my own making, my own childish, childhood fantasy. I had no friends at the shore, and so I created you. Your jealousy and your dreadful visage are nothing but what I imagine you would feel and how you would look. Now go. Go, and never come back."

Angie stood from the cot, her eyes coal black now with pinpoints of flaming red, her lips sneering and her teeth razor-sharp. She pointed a clawed finger that sent sparks into the air. "You betray me, Molly! You create me, you love me, and then you reject and betray me! Beast!"

"Leave, Angie. You are dead to me."

Angie shuddered violently, sparks dancing about her hands and face, and then faded into the shadows of the room. Her voice faded with her — "I am not gone! You are not shed of me! I am not —"

Angie vanished. Molly was alone again with her brother, clutching the sweat-stained letter she had begun to Orville.

She tore the letter up.

Several years passed. Molly continued working at the Triangle Shirtwaist Factory, her grandmother caught a cold and died, Judith married a man who spent his time playing cards with his friends and refused to get a job, and Simon grew tall, heavy, and often violent. And Orville never replied to Molly's notes. Her dreams of flying faded, becoming little more than her memories of catching crabs, riding her bike along sandy roads, and wading in the briny ocean shallows.

Then, on a dreary day in March, Angie appeared in the factory, perched on a chair by the window. And Molly sent her away.

The day was like all others before it. Long, mind-numbing, growing uncomfortably warm with the windows nailed shut. She fed fabric into her machine, creating blouse after blouse. When break time came, Molly ate a biscuit and a slice of cheese, then got back to work. The girls around her did the same, too tired on this

Saturday to chat much, all looking forward to the day's end and the week's pay that awaited them.

Molly folded the blouses in her basket, ready to turn them in to the foreman. As she stood to collect her hat and shawl, Angie was back again, standing at the window. Her hair was wild and flew about her head. Her face, horrible.

"I said you were dead to me, Angie," said Molly. "Leave."

"And I told you I have brought the gift of flight, my dearest," she said, "and I won't be denied." Her voice crackled with fury

"I don't want your gift. I don't need you. Never again, Angie!"

Angie winked her ghastly eyes and wandered over to one of Molly's fellow workers. The girl looked about so as not to be seen, took a draw on the cigarette she'd secretly lit, and then held it down by her side. Angie grinned a spiteful grin then flicked out one clawed finger. The girl, unaware of Angie's presence, felt the air move and she flinched. The cigarette flipped from her hand and landed in a box of oily rags under a nearby table. The girl cursed, looked down and about for the cigarette, then shrugged and put on her cloak.

With a giggle, Angie came back to Molly and put her frosty devil's hands on Molly's shoulders.

"Now," she said, angling her head like a fox sniffing its prey. "It's time to fly."

"What have you done?" Molly asked. At that moment, there was a rushing sound, and flames leapt up from the box, catching the wooden table and the chair next to it and engulfing them. Several girls cried out, "Fire! There's a fire!"

"You've set the factory to fire!" said Molly. She stared at the girl who was once her best friend. A monster leered back at her. "Oh, my God, why did you do that?"

Then girls were rushing around Molly, stumbling, crying, pushing past each other, heading for the door. Smoke followed them like a banshee, filling the room more quickly than water over a crumbled dam. Flames chased the smoke, waves of orange and red, rolling around and through the sewing machines and furniture, baskets of blouses, boxes of material, and barrels of machine oil, setting everything alight.

Molly turned toward the door, but a girl tripped over her and knocked her down. When Molly pulled herself up, fire and smoke had already wrapped around, blocking the way.

One of the foremen grabbed a chair and threw it through the window, shattering the glass and sending in a burst of fresh air which fed the conflagration even more. Girls trapped by the flames rushed for the window.

"The only way out!" one of them cried. "We must jump!"

"Oh, my God!" said Molly.

One by one, weeping girls climbed out through the shattered window, teetered, said quick prayers or crossed themselves, and leapt.

Angie stood beside the window, nodding, smiling, tapping her terrible teeth.

The fire licked Molly's skirt, singed her legs, and she ran to the window to join the others.

"I promised you a gift," said Angie as Molly stepped onto the sill and looked at the shattered, twisted bodies on the street below. "So fly, Molly. Fly away home."

Molly closed her eyes, thought of Orville and the clouds and the briny sea and the cool, fresh winds of Kitty Hawk.

And for a moment, she flew.

The Hole to China
John Everson

The hole was deep enough to step into now. It was slow-going, with his shovel, which was meant more for moving sand than packed grey dirt. He'd broken the edge of it already on a rock that had been hidden in the ground.

Jeremy had started digging the hole on something of a lark two days ago. He'd been sitting there behind the shed, searching for water bugs under the green-stained flagstone piled up near the weedy back fence, when he found the faded blue shovel lying in a patch of weeds. He'd picked it up and used it to dig into the trails of an ant colony at the edge of one of the bits of flagstone, and after he'd unearthed the nursery (and a thousand tiny white eggs), he had just kept on digging.

Tonight after dinner, he'd come back to work on it again. When the yelling began, he simply slipped out the back door of his house and took refuge behind the old rotting wood shed at the back of their lot, just as he had on many nights after his father came home. His parents never noticed. They were too busy threatening to strangle each other.

The spot behind the shed was as far away from the house as he could get and still be in the back yard, which he was forbidden to leave without explicit permission.

He could still hear them inside the house.

Once one of them started, it would go on and on. It made his stomach twist in a particularly unpleasant way. It felt both empty and like he had to throw up at the same time, and he hated it. But nothing he did could get them to stop. He used to try to intervene, begging his parents to stop fighting because they were scaring him, but he either got yelled at, slapped, or sent to his room. Usually all three, actually.

So lately, he'd come out here until the voices in the house quieted or it got too dark to see. Usually the latter happened before the former.

"Whatcha digging there?" a soft voice asked.

Jeremy jumped. He turned to see a woman standing on the other side of the fence. She had long black hair that spilled over her old T-shirt. Freckles spotted her nose and cheeks. She looked older than his mom, but not by a lot. He thought she looked happier than his mom. But that wasn't hard. Nothing ever made his mom happy.

"I didn't mean to startle you," the woman said. "I was just doing a little yardwork and saw you over here."

Jeremy nodded, but didn't say anything. He had never seen the woman before, though she looked friendly enough.

"My name's Roxanne," she said. "But you can call me Roxy for short."

"I'm Jeremy," he said.

"So what are you digging for, Jeremy?" she asked again. "Looking for worms?"

He shook his head. "I'm digging a hole to China," he blurted out.

The woman had a nice smile. When she did, there were all these little crinkles that stretched and made her eyes look happy.

"That's going to take a lot of digging," she said.

He nodded.

"It might be easier to buy a plane ticket," she said.

He shrugged. He didn't have enough money to buy a plane ticket. But he'd heard if you dug far enough, you'd go right through the center of the earth and end up in China. And that would be about as far away from here as he could get... which sounded good to him. It might take a long time, but he had nothing else to do.

"Tell you what," the woman said, leaning closer to him over the fence. "If you want, I can give you a better shovel to use."

Jeremy's face perked up. The blue plastic shovel was kind of a pain. But then he frowned. He wasn't supposed to talk to — or take things — from strangers.

It was almost like the woman read his mind.

"Don't worry," she said. "It's just an old shovel. It used to be my husband's — I got it for him to dig his own hole to China. He left it behind when he went."

She grinned at some private joke and held up a finger. "Wait there, I'll be right back."

She disappeared from view, and Jeremy felt a little uncomfortable. He thought about slipping back around the shed and going back to the house, but at that moment, he heard his mother's voice escalate again. "...care what that *bitch* says, you can just..."

His father's voice crescendoed in answer to mom's shrill taunts. "...shut the hell up! I've got half a mind to..."

Jeremy decided that it was better if he stayed where he was. He wondered how fast he could get to China with the strange woman's shovel. Probably faster than with the old, broken, blue plastic one. He heard her moving things about in the shed next door. He'd never seen her there before; he'd never really seen *anyone* in that back yard before. But he knew the shed. It was older than the one in his yard. You could see the places where

191

the wood was rotting away. The birds had built nests inside it, and sometimes he sat here behind his own shed and watched the birds fly to the roof of the decaying structure next door and disappear inside. There were a couple of missing shingles and you could see the dark spots where the wood had gone soft, letting the sparrows peck their way in.

"Here you go," the woman said, interrupting his contemplation of the neighboring shed's rotten roof. He hadn't seen her pop back up at the fence line, but she was holding a small spade with a wooden handle. The part used for digging into the earth was polished and shiny.

"That looks like gold," Jeremy said, taking the proffered shovel from her hands, and lifting it to look closer at the exceptionally clean metal that was supposed to get dirty with earth.

"It's copper," she corrected. "It's very strong, and it's perfect for working in the earth. It can be your bridge from here to China!"

"Wow, thanks," Jeremy said, unable to take his eyes off the garden implement. "But I don't know..."

"It's not doing anyone any good in my shed," the woman said. "Use it whenever you want to dig, and when you're done, just set it back on this side of the fence, right here," she said, pointing at a spot to the right of an overgrown mulberry bush that dropped so many berries in the summer that the grass near the fence turned purple.

"Okay," he said slowly, but his face still betrayed his unsurety.

"Don't even worry about cleaning it off," she said. "I'll do that before I put it away in the shed. I'm just happy someone else will get some use out of it."

The woman's face beamed at him; her lips were wide and the freckles made her look as if she was a girl just about to laugh. "Dig your way to where you want to go," she said softly, and then slipped away from the fence.

Jeremy took the shovel to his hole and pushed the spade into the earth. It seemed almost a crime to get that perfectly burnished tip muddy, but after the first couple shovelfuls came out of the ground, he didn't worry about that too much. He couldn't believe how much better this was than using his plastic hand shovel. The spade seemed to cut right into the earth like a spoon into mashed potatoes. In five minutes he had moved as much earth as it had taken him to move in an hour with the hand shovel. The hole was growing wider and deeper, and now when he stood in it, his belt was below the edge of the ground.

"Jeremy!" his mother called. He heard the back door slam, which meant she had stepped out on the patio. He climbed out of the hole and hurriedly set the shovel back over the fence where the woman had instructed. He hoped it would still be there to use tomorrow. He hated to give it back so quickly, but he knew the meaning of that voice: time to go in, clean up, and get ready for bed.

"Jeremy, get in here!"

It had gotten dark over the past few minutes — he hadn't even realized. But now he could see the moon peering through the violet sky just over the top of the roof next door. Jeremy took one last look at the hole, and then turned to walk toward the house, where his mom was waiting.

He wished he could just stay out here, and sleep in the hole.

* * *

The shovel was still there on Tuesday night, which was good because the arguments started before dinner was even on the table. Mom spit nasty words under her breath that he knew he wasn't supposed to say and Dad pantomimed strangling her when she turned her back.

Jeremy wolfed down his spaghetti and asked to be excused from the table.

Mom's cheeks were flushed and she nodded quickly; he didn't waste a second slipping off his seat and setting the plate on the counter.

Thanks to the shovel, by the time it got dark, he had dug down three more feet. It was getting difficult to get the dirt out of the hole now, because the edge of the ground was now above his head.

"I'm going to have to dig some stairs," he said to himself. If he went any lower, he wouldn't be able to pull himself out of the hole!

He started slicing furrows into the existing walls, and slowly carved out four stairs into the existing sides of the hole, so that he could step up them and dump the dirt out onto the growing mound along the back of the shed. After stepping up and down them a few times, he realized that he needed something else.

A bucket.

Half the dirt was falling off his shovel by the time he got it above ground. He needed something to put it in. And then he could get more dirt out than just a shovelful at a time.

Jeremy climbed out of the hole and went to his dad's shed. There were lots of buckets in there; he picked out the biggest one he could find — an old white one that used to hold tar or something for the driveway. It had a long silver handle and should be able to hold several shovelfuls at a time. He heard his parents' voices echoing in the shed. They weren't whispering anymore.

"*...frigid bitch...*" "*...perverted asshole...*"

There was a lump in his throat as he heard things he knew he wasn't supposed to. It scared him when they got this way, which happened more and more these days. Once upon a time, the fights had been infrequent, a hot blow-up now and then, and the rest of the time, dad had rolled around on the floor with him and mom had made dinner, kissed both of them and called them her boys.

It seemed like a long time since she'd done that.

Jeremy closed the shed door and walked back around it to the hole carrying the bucket. He tossed it down into the dirt and picked up the shovel, intending to follow.

"How's it going?"

It was Roxanne. She was leaning on the fence; a long lock of kinked black hair trailed over to rest against the grey wooden slats on his side.

"Hello, Miss Roxanne," he said. Mom had always taught him to address adults as miss and mister.

"Just Roxy, please," she said. Today she was wearing glasses — they were sort of squarish, and had emerald arms that disappeared into her hair. Roxy stared at him over the top of the glasses. Her eyes were brown, and he thought she looked amused, somehow.

"How deep did you get?"

Jeremy smiled. "I'll show you!" he said, and stepped into the hole. He was proud of how far he'd dug during the past two evenings. He stepped down his newly carved stairs and disappeared temporarily from sight. Then he popped back up, just bringing his head above ground.

"You look like a gopher," Roxy said with a laugh.

Jeremy laughed. "Can gophers dig all the way to China?"

"Maybe," she said. "It depends how much they want to get there."

"I want to get there."

The smile seemed to slip from her face just a little bit, and she nodded. "I know," she said quietly. "You just keep using my shovel whenever you need it. You'll get where you want to go."

The dirt slipped under his feet just then, and Jeremy

stepped down a stair to regain his balance. When he
stepped back up, Roxy was gone.

* * *

On Friday night, Jeremy's dad didn't come home.
Mom ordered pizza for dinner, and they sat at the table
in silence. Jeremy kept looking at the empty chair to his
right.

"Where's dad?" he asked finally.

"Hopefully six feet under," his mom said, and
shoved another bite into her mouth. It looked to Jeremy
like she was attacking her food, not simply eating it. He
didn't ask any more questions.

Without dad, the house was quiet. Jeremy felt his
stomach work itself into knots; somehow the silence was
even worse than the yelling. He stole back out to the yard
and found the copper shovel waiting for him again on
the other side of the fence. It looked as if Miss Roxy had
cleaned it for him; the blade was gleaming in the fire of
the sunset.

There were now thirteen steps leading down into the
hole. Instead of going straight down, it had to kind of
angle its way deeper and deeper, to allow for the steps.
But he was making progress. It was like he entered
another world when he stepped all the way down the
bottom of the hole. The sky grew farther away and the air
was cooler. Damp. Sometimes dirt fell from the walls and
landed on his neck, making him shiver and jump. He
wasn't the only one working down here. Bugs were busy
digging holes too. They scurried about on the walls,
ducking in and out of tiny tunnels in the earth. He didn't
mind working alongside them, so long as they kept to
themselves.

Jeremy thrust the spade down hard into the dirt. He
came back with a big hunk of dirt and dropped it into the
white bucket. Without pause, he shoved the spade down

again. He wanted to get to China more than ever now. A tear ran down his cheek and he rubbed it angrily away on his sleeve.

The bucket filled up fast.

He picked it up and hefted it step by step to dump out above on the growing mound. It was almost a relief to get back down to the bottom of the hole. He felt safer here. It was his own space. Nobody yelled or did bad things to each other here... because... it was just him.

Jeremy hefted the bucket up the steps a half-a-dozen times. It was starting to get dark outside; the sun had disappeared behind the houses, and there was a faint breeze ruffling the leaves of the trees around him. He looked towards his house. The lights were on in the kitchen, but there were no voices coming from inside. The quiet was refreshing... but eerie. Jeremy wondered where his dad had gone. Maybe he'd decided to go to China, too. But he'd probably get there a lot faster since he'd driven away in their Ford Escort. Driving had to be faster than digging.

"How's it going?"

Roxy was there at the fence again.

Jeremy shrugged. "OK, I guess. I think it's going to take a really long time to do this though," he said.

"I think you're closer than you think," she said.

"But China is all the way on the other side of the world, and I'm still just a few steps down."

Roxy smiled. "I'll tell you a secret. There is a whole network of tunnels beneath our feet that leads to wherever it is you want to go. I think your hole has almost reached them. And once it does... you can go to China... or anyplace else you want. As long as you really want it."

"I do," he said. "I want to be anyplace but here."

Roxy nodded. "Then I'll let you get back to it. Right now — when the day is gone but the night is not quite here? That in-between time? That's the best time for digging to where you're going."

She grinned, and Jeremy could see her freckles bunch up around her nose. "Good luck," she said. Then she walked away, through the tall grass in the yard behind his.

Jeremy stepped down into the hole again, carrying the white bucket. He thought about what Miss Roxy had said, and pushed the shovel into the dark earth near his feet. He might be close! The thought made him dig faster. And he filled the white bucket in no time. The dirt trickled over the edge of the rim, and he decided to try to put one more shovelful on top. He pushed the spade in once more, and this time, when he put his foot on the copper edge of the spade, it sunk down easily into the ground. When he brought it back up, there was dirt on the shovel... and a hole where the spade had been. A hole that went much deeper than the little bit of dirt he'd lifted out.

He pushed the shovel in near the edge, to widen the hole, and as he did, chunks of earth broke away and fell into the blackness below.

"I bet this is one of the tunnels Miss Roxy was talking about," he whispered. He moved around the hole in an ever-widening spiral, shoving the spade down and letting the earth fall away. In just a few minutes, he was looking at a four-foot-wide hole that went... nowhere.

Well, it went somewhere, he supposed. But he wasn't sure just where. Everything below his feet was black... but when he laid on the ground and looked down, he could see stars. Faint pinpricks of light in the darkness below. If he dove through the hole... he'd be in space!?

"You made it," a voice said behind him. Jeremy jumped. She'd surprised him again. Miss Roxy was standing there behind him. Her feet were on the last step.

"It's outer space down there," he said.

Miss Roxy shook her head. "It's whatever you want it to be. If you want to go to China, just picture it in your head, and jump into the hole. That's where you'll go."

"Did your husband go to China?" Jeremy asked.

She shook her head. "I dug the hole for him, and then when he could see the stars, I asked him what he thought hell looked like. He thought about it for a minute, and then described a really horrible place full of fire and impaling spikes and…" Miss Roxy stopped speaking for a moment and shook her head. "Things you don't need to know. When I was sure he had a good picture in his head, I gave him a little push, and away he went. I hope he did end up in the place he imagined… he was a bad, bad man."

"I don't want to go to hell," Jeremy whispered, scooting back from the edge.

"No, no, sweetie, I would never have given you the shovel for that. I want you to go where you want to go."

"I want to go to China," Jeremy said. He stood up, his eyes welling with tears. "I don't want to be here anymore."

Miss Roxy nodded. Her face was serious. "Think of China, then," she said. "Close your eyes and picture it really good in your mind."

Jeremy screwed his eyes shut and held them that way. In his head, he imagined the place that he'd been thinking about for months every night when he laid down to sleep. In his mind, there were beautiful, tall buildings with flags and banners waving in the wind. Horses marched along stone paths and dogs frolicked in the grassy square. All around him, short people walked hand in hand. Hardly anyone was taller than Jeremy, but everyone was friendly and kind.

"Do you see it?" Miss Roxy asked softly.

Jeremy nodded, but didn't open his eyes.

"Good," she said. "Just take a step forward, and you'll be there."

"I'm afraid," he whispered.

Miss Roxy put her hand on his shoulder. "Is the place you're thinking of nice?"

He nodded.

"Is it where you want to go?"

He nodded again, faster.

"Then I'll help you," she said, and gave him a gentle push.

* * *

When Jeremy's mother stopped yelling out the back door for him, and instead stepped out of the house and into the back yard, she immediately walked to the shed. She knew Jeremy had been digging back there lately. She'd let him do it since it kept him out of her hair.

"Jeremy!" she yelled, stepping around the back. "You are *so* going to be grounded."

But when she turned the corner to the back of the shed, Jeremy wasn't there. The evidence of what he'd been doing remained, however — a mound of dirt was piled up near the fence, and the hole in the ground where it had come from was nearby. It looked as if Jeremy had dug down two or three feet in the dirt. The broken blue plastic shovel he'd apparently been using lay abandoned next to the hole.

She called her son's name once more, and looked around at the rest of the yard, and then at the neighbor's house next door. The place was overgrown with weeds; nobody had actually lived there since the murder, years ago. After the wife had gone missing, the police had questioned the husband, but never came up with enough evidence to arrest him. When they had finally come around with dogs, they'd unearthed the body of his wife, found buried beneath the floor of the broken-down shed. Ironically, by the time they discovered the whereabouts of the missing wife, the husband had gone missing. And he had never been found. Most people assumed he'd fled the country to avoid being arrested.

Jeremy's mother shivered in the breeze and looked up at the old, empty house next door. It may have been a trick of the rising moon… but there appeared to be a face in the upstairs window. A woman's face.

The woman seemed to be smiling.

Jeremy's mother looked away and around the darkening yard once more, calling angrily for her son. When she glanced back at the window of the house next door, the woman had vanished.

Just like her husband.

Just like her son.

She stared at the hole Jeremy had begun to dig. She remembered when she was a kid, how the other kids used to say that if you dug down in your back yard really deep, you could dig all the way to China. Once in her life, she'd really believed that was true. Once, she'd believed a lot of things were true.

A tear crept down her face, followed quickly by another.

God, did she wish she still believed that now.

She wished she could dig a hole to take her far away from here.

All the way to China.

She Sits And Smiles
Chet Williamson

The old woman sat in the hall. Her room was near the nurses' station, so anyone going down the hall had to pass by her. She didn't talk. She didn't talk at all anymore, not even to the nurses who took care of her and helped her with her meals and her toilet. She simply sat in the chair and smiled.

When morning came, after she had been fed her breakfast, she dragged a metal chair with a green plastic padded seat and back from her room into the hall and placed it against the wall next to her door. It took her a long time. She walked backwards, her hands on the back of the chair so that it supported her as she moved. She would take two steps backward, drag the chair toward her, lean on it for a moment as if to regain her strength, and then repeat the action until both she and the chair were in the hall. Then she would take a few steps to the side, dragging the chair along, until she was clear of the doorway. Painstakingly, she turned the chair around until it faced her, and maneuvered her way down onto the seat. Once there, she sat and she smiled.

"Why does she smile so much?" Becca Riley asked Ron Knapp as they sat in the break room. It was Becca's first week on the job. "If I had to have somebody help me eat and…well, you know… I wouldn't be smiling all the time."

"She's just got a positive attitude," Ron said. "I've seen it before, even in cases like hers where life hardly seems worth living, but she just smiles and gets through it."

Becca shook her head. "She doesn't even watch TV…doesn't read…you ever hear her talk?"

"No, and I've been here three years. All I've seen her do is drag out that chair, sit in the hall, and smile at people when they go by."

"It kinda creeps me out," Becca said, then finished the rest of her coffee. "So how can she drag out that chair, but not feed herself?"

"Fine motor skills are shot. Her hands shake too much," Ron said. "Still, she could be a lot worse. I mean, what does she do? She sits and smiles. That's nice, y'know?"

They left the break room and walked down the hall, past the old woman. She smiled at them as they went by. Ron smiled back. Becca didn't. She looked away as soon as the old woman's gaze fell on her. In spite of that, it was still Ron who the old woman wanted to kill.

She always had wanted to kill the nice ones, the ones who went out of their way to be helpful or kind. It had always been that way, even with the tramps. The friendly ones, those who offered to do some yard work for their handouts, they were the ones she hated, the ones she wanted to kill. They just got on her nerves. The bitter ones, those who had been crushed down by life, the ones any other woman would have been scared of and have shut the door on, those were the ones she *liked*. Because they were more like her, she supposed. She liked them because they wore the faces that she couldn't wear. Smiles were the *false* faces. Masks. When she saw a smile, she saw a lie, the same lies that her own smile told. So what she did to Ron as a result was what she had done before. To those who smiled.

She took him out to the shed, the small one with the thick walls that Daddy had used as an icehouse in summer. She didn't have to come up with an excuse, not any more. He followed her, and when she opened the heavy door, he entered in front of her. She went in behind him, taking the mallet from its place just inside the door, and hit him in the back of the head with it. He fell with a little moan.

She closed the door behind them, tightly, so that the felt edges slipped into place against the jamb. She didn't have to light the lantern the way she did before. There was enough light now, all the light she wanted. She didn't know where it came from, but it shone brightly wherever she wanted it to, illuminating her work. Her eyes were old and tired, and clouds passed in front of her gaze more often than not, but here in the shed her sight was as clear as when she was a child, and the colors were rich and deep, especially the reds. There were so many different kinds of reds, shades she'd never before seen, all beautiful.

She wouldn't have had to close the door either. Before, she always had so that the screams wouldn't be heard, but there was no one to hear now. Still, she kept it closed, partly out of habit, and partly because the shed felt snug and safe with it closed, and she liked that feeling. It made her happy. It made her smile for real, a smile that wasn't a lie or a mask.

She took the ropes from the corner and tied Ron to the posts that were firmly planted in the dirt floor. There were four of them, positioned so that Ron was spread-eagled when she was done. She didn't have to hurry the way she had before, because she knew that Ron would remain unconscious until it was time for him to be awake, time for him to feel what was happening to him.

Her hands worked swiftly nonetheless, her fingers no longer bent and crackling with arthritis, but deftly interweaving the cords around the wrists and ankles and posts, knotting them tightly, with all the strength of the young farm woman she had been.

There, now she was done. He could wake up now, and he did. His eyes widened when he saw her standing there, holding the pair of tin snips Daddy had used to trim and repair the corrugated metal roofs on some of the outbuildings. They went through cloth like a hot poker through lard, even the tough denim of Ron's jeans. She cut off his clothes carefully, though. She didn't want him to bleed yet. But she put the heavy blades of the tin snips against his flesh plenty of times. She liked feeling him wince, and she liked the little catches of breath that he made.

Finally he was naked, and she sat down on a small wooden stool to observe what she had done. She had no idea of how long she had taken to cut off his clothes. Time had no dominion here in the shed. But she knew that what would happen next would take a luxuriously long time. Their fear was good, but their pain was much better.

But many of them started to beg even before the pain began, and Ron was one of those. He asked her to please let him go, and she watched him and said nothing, did nothing but sit and smile. Then he asked her, as nearly every one of them did, why she was doing this. This she could answer him, and she did, without opening her mouth or speaking aloud. He heard her words.

Because I can. Because I want to. Because I like it.

He started to cry then, and she got off the stool and knelt next to him. She lowered her lips to his eyes and cheeks and tasted his tears. They were like all the others, salty and warm and delicious. She put her face against him so that her lips were on his, and her upper lip was wet with the mucus that ran from his nose as he cried. His breath came in pants, and she welded her mouth to his, inhaling, sucking in his air so that he was forced to breathe through his dripping nostrils, until she pinched his nose shut with her fingers. He twisted his head, trying to move it to the side to free himself from her breath-stealing kiss, but she was much stronger than he, and held his head in place until she felt him start to go limp beneath her. Then she yanked her head away, and their mouths separated as air rushed into his throat and his body bucked with the effort of breathing. His pupils, which had rolled up into his head, reappeared, and he blinked as the air wheezed in and out of his starving lungs.

She smiled and sat on the stool again. Ron continued to breathe, gradually calming until he was looking at her again. Then she decided it was time to take off her clothes. She knew that it didn't matter if the blood or anything else splattered on her clothing. There was no need to cover up anything anymore, no need to worry about a stray drop of blood on her blouse or a piece of flesh stuck in her hair. But being naked brought her closer to the experience, intensified it as it had in the past. So she slowly undressed, letting Ron watch as she revealed her round belly, her strong, heavy arms and legs, her pendulous breasts and the other woman part of her, bristling with thick, dark hair.

He looked scared, frightened of the sheer physicality of her, and she preened and even strutted for a time to heighten his fear. Then she got down to work. From the corner she took her box of tools — blades, files, chisels, punches, all from Daddy's workshop. There were a tremendous number of implements, but over long years she had decided upon four that seemed to work best, to easily produce the reactions and responses that most delighted her. She knelt by Ron and began to play.

It was some time later that Becca Riley once again passed the old woman in the hall. When she was several yards away, Becca noticed with relief that the woman was not looking in her direction. Her eyes seemed focused on the opposite wall, and she was smiling the way she always did. But even though Becca had increased the speed of her pace to pass the old woman quickly, when she was only a few feet away from her, she slowed. Something was holding her back, as though the air had thickened and solidified around the old woman. At last Becca stopped. And she saw.

It was only a glimpse, but it was as clear as it had been when she was in college and Dave Purvis had shown up at her dorm for a date. When she had come into the lobby, he had been sitting waiting for her, but he was looking down, distracted, and when she was a few feet away from him, when she entered what she later thought of as the orbit of his thoughts, she had had the same kind of glimpse within Dave's mind that she now had within the old woman's, and for merely a split second she saw Dave doing something to her, something terrible, with no love or affection attached to it, only hatred for her and for all other women.

She had turned red, stammered, but finally told Dave that she wasn't feeling well and would have to cancel. Fury had sparked in his eyes, but he smiled and tried to make another date. She had tentatively agreed, then emailed him later to cancel again. Four months later, just before summer break, he had date-raped and beaten a sophomore Becca did not know.

And now, for the first time since the incident with Dave, and for the second time in her life, she had that sensation again, that feeling of a bright light shining into a darkened cellar, exposing things that should remain hidden. She saw through the old woman's eyes, or rather through her mind, and what she saw was Ron Knapp, his face streaked with tears and blood, lined with slashes, the flesh of his chest peeled back like an orange, and fingers, the old woman's fingers, digging between the yellow rib bones, pressing into the gray-green bags of the lungs. What Becca heard was something she never wanted to hear again, but knew that she would, both waking and sleeping.

The sight and the sound lasted only an instant, then it was gone, and the old woman jerked her dumb gaze from the blank wall and looked at Becca. Her smile vanished for a moment. When it did, Becca saw in the old woman's expression something even worse than the vision she felt certain they had shared.

Then the smile returned, winked back on as though, Becca thought, the woman had slapped a mask over her face. The old woman sat there, her head turned, smiling at Becca, who recoiled at the thought of getting any closer to the raddled body whose brain held such awful images. Becca pressed herself against the opposite wall to edge past the old woman, whose smiling gaze followed her, as did the strand of spittle that dangled from the drooping underlip.

By the time Becca was past her, the woman seemed to forget about her. Her sparsely haired head slowly rolled back until she was looking once again at the wall, still smiling, apparently lost in thought.

She was back in the shed now, with the saw. It was time to finish her fun. Before, by the time it got to this point, they were gone. They could no longer see and feel and hear. But now it was so much better. Even skinned like Daddy's rabbits, they could still watch and feel as the saw tore through what flesh she had left them before reaching the bone, could hear the rasp of it as it chewed into the tough white sticks that held thigh to hip, shoulder to neck. And they could still whine and whimper and scream, even as she was sawing through

211

the many small bones of the neck, and they had no air left to scream.

Surrounded by the various pieces of Ron Knapp, she stood naked, the saw in her hand, blood coating her bare flesh, admiring what she had done — the feet and calves and thighs, the fingers and hands and wrists and forearms and upper arms, all robustly if not neatly separated. The disassembled torso, with the many pieces of flesh and all the parts that made up a person inside, things whose names she had never known, except for a few, like heart and stomach and bowels and liver. There were other small ones that confused her, but they were interesting to pluck out just the same, and she laughed when she did.

Ron's head was the closest piece to her, and his eyes still looked up at her majesty, his mouth still opened and closed. She picked up the head, steadied it between her breasts, and plucked out the eyes, then pulled open the jaw until it cracked, and the mouth stopped moving. She tossed it down the way Daddy carelessly tossed away the black, dead stubs of his cigar butts.

Now the hard work was ahead of her, because even here, in this idealized version of her shed, her most happy of places, she didn't feel she could just let these pieces lie on the dirt floor. So she took a deep breath, the smell of the blood and the contents of the unloosed and then opened bowels strong and sweet in her flared and welcoming nostrils, and set to work.

She was stronger and younger now, and she could scoop up the pieces easily. It was amazing how light flesh could be when the life had poured out of it. She carried the various parts of Ron Knapp to where she had always put the rest of them, dropped the pieces on the ground, reached down, and pulled up the door. There was no need for a lock. In they went, down into the ground with the others. When she heard the pieces land, making the bones that were already there rattle and clack, she smiled again. She dropped the door on it all, and, still naked, went back to the hall where she found herself, still clothed, sitting on the metal and plastic chair, staring at the wall. She smiled for a long time at the new memories added to the old, both false and true, until it was time to eat again.

By that time, Becca and Ron's shift was over. During the few days Becca had been employed there, they'd been working side by side, and Becca thought they'd been getting along fine, but not intimately enough for her to tell Ron what she had felt from the old woman, just as she'd never told anyone about what she had assumed to be her psychic confrontation with Dave Purvis. Most people didn't believe in that stuff, and most of those who did were the kind of flakes with whom Becca never hung out.

Still, she knew she had to look further into the old woman's past. She had felt something so strong, so unmistakable, that she knew there had to be something to it. Why would a woman pushing one hundred have such visions — fantasies? — unless there was something in her past to cause them?

But then, complication upon complication, what possible explanation could Becca give to Ron, or to anyone, for her curiosity?

She considered it that night, and the following morning she put her new plan into action. When lunchtime came, Ron usually went to the old woman's room to feed her, but today Becca volunteered to take his place. "She *does* always seem so happy, like you said," Becca told Ron. "Maybe I just need to get to know her a little. That smile might be contagious."

She hated to do it, but she had no choice. Ron helped the old woman back into her room from the hall, and Becca followed with the tray of food. Once the old woman was seated in her chair, Ron left, and Becca set the tray on the wheeled overbed table and slid it in front of the woman, who continued to smile, but kept her eyes fixed on the tray of food rather than on Becca.

Becca spooned some chicken rice soup out of the shallow bowl and held it up to the old woman's mouth. The fissured lips opened, still retaining their smile, and Becca guided the spoonful in. The lips closed, and Becca slid the spoon out as the woman tasted and swallowed. Becca continued her actions mechanically, as did the old woman, who now and again looked at the saltines, which Becca dutifully put between the woman's teeth so she could bite off a shard.

"Do you want to tell me anything?" Becca asked softly, so as not to be heard through the open door to the hall. The woman didn't respond. "About yesterday?" Becca went on. "About what I saw inside your head. About what you were thinking of?"

The old woman kept chewing her cracker. She didn't look at Becca, but then, she didn't seem to be purposely looking away either.

"I did see it, you know." Becca's spoon went into the pudding, which she lifted to the woman's accepting mouth. "Do you care that I saw it?" The woman said nothing. "Don't you care?" Becca asked, so softly that she scarcely heard her own voice.

When the old woman had eaten everything, Becca pushed the overbed table aside, picked up the tray, and walked out of the room. She didn't have to try to appear upset. Her proximity to the old woman had been enough to do that. As she walked up the hall, Ron came toward her. "Everything go all right?" he asked.

"No," Becca said. "Does she...ever talk to you?" Ron shook his head. "She did to me," Becca said, not fully lying.

"It was…fragmented," Becca told Ron later in the break room. "I don't recall the exact words, but it had to do with, well, death."

"A lot of people her age think about death — talk about it sometimes."

"Not *her* death," Becca said. "Other people. She said…'I killed.' A number of times."

"Now wait," Ron interrupted. "She said she *killed?*" He shook his head. "I've never heard her utter a word. Why the hell would she…"

"I don't know," Becca said. "But that's what she said. And she looked…I don't know…*happy* about it."

"Well…how did it come up? I mean, how did she start talking at all?"

Becca shrugged. "She just did. She looked right at me and she said she *killed*. She wasn't very clear. It was as though she hadn't spoken for a long time. But there were a few other words too…'blood'…and 'men,' or maybe 'man,' I'm not sure. Some other words I couldn't make out."

Ron looked at Becca, then down at the tabletop. "This is crazy," he said. "What would make her…" The words trailed off.

"What do you know about her?" Becca asked.

What Ron didn't know, they found out together from the nursing home's files and from the people who had worked there longer than Ron had. The old woman had lived her entire life on a nearby farm. Her mother had died in childbirth, and her father died when he was in his forties. She had no siblings, and never married. After her father's death, she rented some of the farmland to tenant farmers, and, over the years, sold off much of the land to developers.

When she was in her mid-eighties, she became unable to care for herself and had to enter the nursing home, where she had resided for fifteen years. Before she did, she sold off the remainder of the land, keeping only a half acre on which the farmhouse, barn, and sheds still stood. A trust fund established with the final development money paid for the annual taxes on the property, which was to go to the nursing home upon her death.

"So no one's probably been in that place since she left it," Becca said to Ron as they walked together to the parking lot, after they'd learned everything they could. "I think we should...go out there."

"Y'know," Ron said with a frustrated sigh, "maybe she was just talking about killing chickens. She did live on a farm, after all. They killed their meat."

"She wasn't," Becca said, leaning against her car, washed yellow by the mercury vapor lights. "She meant more than that."

"How do you know? And even if she did, how do you know it wasn't just a fantasy? Old people, they think...talk crazy things sometimes."

Becca looked into Ron's face. She made her eyes go as hard and cold as she could. "I *know*, Ron. Please trust me, but I know. I looked into her eyes, and I saw...well..." She shook her head. "Just go out there with me. If we find nothing, no harm done. It'll take an hour, tops. Please."

The next day was Sunday, a day off for both of them. Becca drove, and Ron navigated. They went early, hoping not to draw the attention of people who lived nearby. Anyone who was up at eight o'clock would probably be headed to church, or so Becca hoped.

There were housing developments where Becca assumed the farmland had been, but as they drew nearer to the farm itself, the developments contracted into mini-estates, and the individual lots grew larger, as did the houses. By the time they spied the three-story height of the barn ahead, all that was around them were fields, still undeveloped in the economy that had crippled the state for the past several years.

As they drove back the dirt road that led to the farm, Becca saw a classic two-story farmhouse near the barn, with three other outbuildings of various sizes, all of which were in need of paint. A hundred yards down the road, they were stopped by an eight-foot-high chain link fence that surrounded the buildings. A heavy, rusted padlock was on a gate.

"Now what?" Ron asked. "I don't think we should break in."

Becca pulled the parking brake and turned off the ignition. "Let's look around."

A light rain had started, and she pulled up the hood of her sweatshirt. They walked around the perimeter, and at one of the rear corners found that a pole had rusted through to the extent that all they had to do was pull the fencing away, and they could slip through.

Becca led the way to the house first. The front door was locked. They tried to look through the windows, but when they wiped away the dust from the outside of a pane, they discovered that it was nearly as dirty on the inside. Becca fished her phone from her pocket and turned on the LED app, but the light merely reflected off the dusty surface, and Becca stood on the porch, frowning.

"You're not suggesting we break a window," Ron said, half seriously.

"No." She shook her head. "This isn't right anyway."

"Huh?"

Becca tried to remember what she had seen in the old woman's head, not the details of what was being done to Ron Knapp, but the overall presence of the imagined place, the *ambiance* of it, and then she recalled, ever so teasingly, what had framed the image of Ron, like recalling the dark background of a Rembrandt portrait.

217

Earth. Dirt, darkened perhaps with blood, and she knew that wherever the old woman had taken Ron in her mind, it had not been inside the house, unless the cellar had a dirt floor. Still, on a farm there were other possibilities, and she walked down the porch steps toward the sheds.

The one that claimed her attention was the farthest from the house, and the only one that had no windows. Becca walked around it, Ron in her wake. It was raining harder now, and her hood was soaked through. She examined the door, and saw edges of something that looked like heavy felt all around the frame. "Here," she whispered.

There was a large padlock on the door, but the hinges were held by rusty screws. Becca took a Swiss Army knife from her pocket and opened the screwdriver blade. "What are you doing?" Ron asked, sounding alarmed.

"Taking out a hinge just enough to pull back the door and look in."

"Jesus…" Ron hunched his shoulders against the rain. "That thing hasn't been opened in years."

Becca didn't respond to the obvious. One by one, she loosened the four screws of the upper hinge, putting them in her pocket so they could be reinserted. "There," she said, pocketing the final screw. "Now let's see…just pull this back far enough for me to look through and shine my light in…"

Ron worked his fingers around the top corner of the thick door and pulled gently outward. A wedge of blackness appeared, and from it there came an odor that made both of them wince. Ron released his grip, and the door slammed itself back into place.

"Jesus," he muttered, looking at Becca with wide eyes.

"Again," Becca said, and thumbed her phone to the LED app.

They both set their faces against the smell that would plunge out at them, and Ron reluctantly dug his fingers into the soft wood and pulled. The reeking odor reasserted itself, their expectation making it no less horrible. It smelled rank, salty, sweet-sour, rotten, like blood and shit and rent bowels. The wider Ron made the gap, the more of the stench poured out. Becca heard Ron gag deep in his throat, but by then she was leaning past him, shining the white-hot LED light into the shed and peering through the crack with one eye.

The cyclopean view allowed for only two dimensions, and for that she was grateful. The sight was awful enough on a flat plane. The floor of the shed was dirt, but at the center, in the area defined by four heavy posts, the dirt was reddish-brown, becoming lighter toward the perimeter. There were bits of what Becca could only imagine was flesh scattered about, glinting in the light's beam as though still retaining traces of moisture. It was, she thought, a scene of slaughter, but what was most surprising was that the slaughter seemed recent.

She pulled herself away from the door and nodded to Ron to let it fall back into place. "We need to call the police," was the first thing she said. Then she told him what she had seen.

As pale as he had become, he grew paler still, so that she feared he might topple over. But he remained upright, and then nodded.

One police car came, and after the shed had been opened and the officers found tools with blood and bits of organic matter clinging to them, more cars joined it. Becca told them what she had told Ron about the old woman speaking to her, and she and Ron were taken to the local justice of the peace for further questioning, so they did not see the discovery that occurred at mid-afternoon, when the rain had stopped.

The police found a slightly sunken area three feet by two feet that grass had grown over, and when they cleared away the turf and two inches of earth, they found a trap door that opened down into an old septic tank. The trap door had rusted shut and had to be opened with a crowbar.

Inside the septic tank was a vast assortment of human bones. When they were examined, it was found that some of the bones had probably been in the tank for over sixty years. But despite the evidence that the trap had not been opened in at least a decade, some of the bones were much newer, with organic tissue still clinging to them, as fresh and moist as the shards of flesh that were found on the dirt floor of the shed.

The old woman never explained. She never uttered a word. It made no difference to her whether she sat in the hall of the nursing home, or in the hall of this new, far grayer building to which they had taken her. Every day after breakfast, she dragged her chair into the hall. This chair was plastic, not metal, but it was fine. It was something to sit on, and she sat and she smiled at everyone who walked by. And those who smiled back were the ones she took to the shed. They were the ones whose bones she dropped into the earth.

Carry On, Carrion
Paula D. Ashe

Children are curious, inquisitive; their minds —
while delusional — are more receptive to the true nature
of things. As such, the kids who creep along the sides of
my crumbling home to catch a glimpse of "Melty Face"
sometimes catch a glimpse of something more.
Something that makes their immature understanding,
their nascent reasoning, recoil in inarticulate terror.

After seeing me, one particularly perceptive twelve-
year-old went home, ate dinner with his family, played
video games with his younger brother, brushed his teeth
and washed his face, and — so his parents thought —
went to bed. The next morning, Cameron awoke before
his parents and brother. In the dark, he poured himself a
bowl of cereal, then added milk. Previously, the bowed
shape of the spoon fit the musculature of his mouth like a
hand sliding into a glove. Now, the object was no longer
a utensil, but a dysfunctional deterrent to his purposes.

His father saw him first. In his bleary state, the man
didn't notice the black blotches of blood and tissue
trailing from the bathroom into the kitchen. His patent
leather slippers squelched on slick bits of flesh and
ground the gore into the recently cleaned carpet.
Cameron dropped his useless spoon and gulped down

his breakfast while thin cascades of pink milk dribbled from the corners of his red, red mouth. The scream woke the rest of the family.

I watched from my attic window while an ambulance carried Cameron away on a stretcher. They'd bandaged him up, stuck tubes and needles in him, tried to protect the neighbors from his revelatory act by holding up a sheet on either side of him. From my elevated vantage point, however, I saw the boy.

He'd shaved away his mask and in that moment, I was proud.

After the paramedics took Cameron and his family to the hospital and the lookie-loos remembered their own children inside their homes unattended, I snuck inside to see Cameron's story scrawled raw on rubicund walls.

I found the spoon still on the kitchen floor. A talisman, I slid it into my mouth and the sweet, milky taste of his ripening trilled delightfully along my ganglia.

The bathroom became an abattoir. Scattered around the sink I found discarded strips of skin wrapped messily in balls of tissue paper. The gesture made my heart hurt. I stood in front of the mirror and searched my scabrous reflection while imagining Cameron's compulsion. He saw the parasitic shroud and could no longer bear its morbid weight, but he also recognized the sentimental value held by the collection of inherited features. So that he didn't discard them, he saved them as a sort of keepsake for a family that would see him only as forever ruined.

Above the boy's bed I scrawled the sigil into the wall with the edge of the spoon's handle. Once Cameron and the family return, when the dark reaches its umbral peak, the Man with a Face of Teeth will come.

As he came to me.

* * *

It was a desolate September night. The moon loomed bright and large and clear. A great
silver menace; radiating cold hatred, revealing weird atmospheres of bone-colored stars and gas-green heavens.

My car sat like a lone ship in a vast pavement ocean.

The strap of my bag dug into my shoulder. Heavy with shit essays to grade and notebooks of my own shit to provide some kind of balance; shifting the bag to grab my keys, I pushed the button to unlock the door then tossed the bag into the passenger seat.

A sharp, stainless kiss near my ankle. It was then I realized I had always been waiting for doom. Should have checked underneath the car. Should have carried my keys in a tight fist to claw the metal prongs across my assailant's demented face. Should have had someone from security walk me out; that one big guy, possibly slow. Stan? Sam? The back of his head is as flat as a cutting board. Should have parked out front. Should have taken another job. Should have been born male.

Should have, should have.

Instead of looking down I looked up. What was the point, right? There was someone underneath my car. They'd been waiting. They stuck me with something. A sedative smothered the panic scorching my insides. Why be afraid?

Why?

Because I looked up.

And in the moonless sky shone a face made of white teeth.

* * *

"Welcome to the Carcass House."

Slow-surfacing in a soft sea. A bright blob of light. Immobile while the waves danced. The light had a face.

225

. Pain. Pain like a lens, drew my nerves into synaptic focus. I preferred the blur.

"Welcome to the Carcass House."

* * *

The place was damp. The air cold, yet thick with fluid. I sat tied to a wooden chair. To my right was a hallway lit by a bare bulb. Before the hallway was a small room with dingy paint peeling from the walls and what looked like dirty red shag carpeting. Two legs jutted out from behind the doorframe. Obnoxious sneakers and tight, hipster jeans the color of pink chalk. Some kid. My heart skipped a beat, then thundered.

A kid.

CLOMP CLOMP CLOMP

The room shook and my muscles seized. They remembered something I did not. I closed my eyes. I remembered hearing the sound filtered through fathoms of unconsciousness. Big boots stomped down old wooden stairs. I feigned a stupor and my head lolled onto my right shoulder. I peeked through barely open slits. I didn't lift my head, so I couldn't see – you didn't want to see – his face. From the shoulders down I knew he was my assailant. Broad, muscular, in a mustard-colored sweater, black shirt, and black jeans. He carried something large and mechanical in one titanic hand. Was there a blade on it? An electrical cord trailed behind him.

A stuffed-down scream erupted from the small room. I lifted my head, looked around. What if there were just the three of us? The sneakers were flexing back and forth, right and left, in unison. His legs had to be bound together. I twisted my hands in their bonds. Some kind of plastic fiber, stung like a bitch, rubbed my skin raw. I kept pulling. The sneakers shuddered. Another smothered scream. I rocked against the chair, jerked myself forward. A fiery circlet of pain gnawed into each wrist. Beads of sweat broke across my forehead. The muscles in my arms faintly complained. Shut up, just keep pulling. I realized, foolishly, that my bladder was painfully full. The noose on my right wrist tightened but the left remained the same. My hands were tied onto two different parts of the chair. I couldn't use one to undo the other.

Pull. *Pull.*

The screaming stopped. I looked up, held my breath. I could only see a shadow against the wall opposite the boy with the sneakers. I didn't know how – blame the blasphemous physics of the space – but I heard him inhale, I heard the scream building up in his throat, I anticipated the clamor, but then—

—the sharp whir of an electric saw. Electric metal teeth tore through wet pockets of biological inks. Exposed organs glistened with lurid sheens of chemicals.

His scream went shrill. I closed my eyes. I didn't want to see.

* * *

My assailant pulled the boy out of the room piece by piece and made a pile of him in front of me. I didn't start screaming until he sat the shoes on top of the soggy pile, dribbling noisily against the concrete floor. The man, whose face was still an impossibility I could not and would not acknowledge, clomped back up the stairs.

Alone, I listened to that soft drip until it stopped. The boy's sneakers were stained a deep red, and at their openings peeked the severed stumps of his feet.

I started to laugh. And the force of the laughter pushed the urine out of me. The bright sound echoed against the moldering basement walls. Beneath that sound was the liquid music of elimination.

Me and the boy, dripping together in the dark.

After that, the Man with the Face of Teeth brought me a container of a substance with a smell so corrosive it made my nose run and my eyes sting as soon as he entered the room. He untied me. I didn't even try to run or to clean myself. What difference did it make?

On the surface of the sizzling tub of acid, I watched my reflection warp and bend.

"You know what happens after we die, don't you?"

His reflection nodded.

"It's not the end. That's why you came to me."

He nodded again.

For the first time, I looked up at him. The teeth grew concentrically outward — bicuspids, incisors, canines, molars, around and around and around. There was a tough pink line of tissue that encompassed the point of contact between his dentition and skull. No hair grew past that line, though he had a full head of dark hair. No teeth grew farther than that boundary.

I looked back down at the caustic liquid. If he told me *no* at least I wouldn't have to see it. "While I do this, will you hold my hand?"

I bent over and shoved my face into the chemical.

And the Man with the Face of Teeth slipped his hand into mine.

One Possible Shape Of Things To Come
Brian Hodge

Imagine this going on under your own roof. You'd think it was just you, right?

The scene was a late evening in later summer, the second day of the first visit I'd been able to pay my sister in years, trading northern Colorado for northern California. The second day of a planned six, which, yes, is a risk. That advice about company and fish going bad after three days may hold true for family even more than everyone else.

But we were grown-ups now. That whole pattern of torment and retaliation was behind us. Grown-ups. Meredith more than me, maybe, but we'd always evolved at different rates.

Here's how I knew Meredith was permanently done with glow sticks, whirling her bikini top overhead at pool parties, and yacking up Mike's Hard Lemonade into bushes: For the past five years, her life's orbit had happily revolved around a benign dictator who now stood three-foot-seven and still had to be stopped from eating from the potpourri bowl. Because he insisted it was purple cereal.

Here's how a typical discussion about that would go:

"See that water it's in? We don't pour water over

cereal, do we?" *Unimpeachable logic from his dad, Ethan, my brother-in-law.*

"It's clear milk." *Declared with the unshakable conviction of a CEO.*

"But milk isn't clear." *Your puny logic is doomed to fail, dad-man.*

"Yes it is. It's from see-through cows." *You were warned.*

I loved this kid, my one and only nephew, Micah. He was everything I aspired to be, if only I could still get away with it. One thing I was looking forward to most in the world was being the cool uncle. The unsavory adult he could talk to about things he could never bring up with his parents, and who was going to turn him onto cultural touchstones that would make him a demigod among his friends.

In time. In time.

For now, my visit mostly amounted to medical missionary work with Ethan after the resident five-year-old was in bed. I'd brought along a care package of the sort of things that Ethan, poor bastard, never got to enjoy anymore. Sometimes it's all about saving your fallen brothers.

"It's a Korean revenge flick, that's all you need to know," I told him while loading the disc in the Blu-ray player. Then we reacquainted him with the simple joys of our generation's version of tuning in, turning on, dropping out. Our one concession was using a nebulizer because, if we insisted on getting quietly baked, Meredith didn't want the house smelling like smoke. It wasn't the same, until we just didn't care.

"Jesus," Ethan said a half-hour in. "The Koreans don't fuck around."

"No," I said. "They don't."

"I forgot they made movies like this." He inhaled a hit of mist and looked utterly baffled. "It's all Lion King

and mermaid shit now. At some point you just go numb.
It's either go numb, or realize there's a set number of
times you can hear the same stupid cheerful song before
you hear it telling you to hang yourself. And you don't
want to find that number."

"Easy," I said. "Brook's here. I've got your back. I'm
here to help."

He watched awhile longer. "I'm going to miss you
when you're gone, brother."

None of which was the weird part. Scenes like that
were no doubt going on all over, in millions of homes,
everyone thinking that, a few misgivings aside, all was
right with the world … even though, even then, it wasn't.

We had the movie down and were contemplating
another when Meredith poked her head into the family
room and gave us a sour look that wasn't too harsh, as if,
as reprobates go, we could've been worse.

"You need to see this. Now." It was clear she was
speaking to Ethan and it was obviously about Micah.
"Hurry."

I followed too, both of us adopting my sister's haste-
stealth pace up the carpeted stairs, until the three of us
clustered in Micah's doorway. Ethan peered over her
right shoulder as I peered over her left.

"I just checked in on him, and he was like this," she
whispered. "Should we be worried about this?"

Micah's room was dim, despite the nightlight
burning along one baseboard and the wedge of light
from the hallway's ceiling lamp behind us. His bed was
empty, the covers rumpled and trailing into the floor, as
if they sought to join the scattered toys.

His back was to us, as Micah stood in the far corner,
facing into it with his head tipped halfway down. He was
as motionless as I'd ever seen any kid out of bed.

"What's going on with him?" Meredith whispered.

Ethan slipped past, steering around the toys until he

was at Micah's knobby little shoulder. "Hey. Buddy? Shouldn't you be in bed?"

No response, and by now, my sister was there too. "Micah? Why are you standing in the corner?"

I thought he wasn't going to respond to that, either, that maybe he'd been sleepwalking and didn't hear them. Then he turned his head to look back at us, and awake or not, everything was still slowed down, dreamlike, his voice a flat monotone.

"I've been bad," he said.

Both Meredith and Ethan told him no, no, he hadn't been bad, and this was true, he hadn't really misbehaved during the entire time I'd been there. Regardless, he shook his head with great slowness and terrible weight, as if the matter were settled.

"They told me to wait here," he said.

"*Who* told you?" Meredith asked.

Back to the silent treatment. He wasn't answering that one.

"Wait for what?" Ethan said.

"To be punished."

As they steered him back to his bed, Micah went willingly, seeming to let it happen rather than under his own steam, and they tucked him in tight, cinching him down with more covers than he needed in late summer. He fell asleep immediately, if he'd even been awake at all, and they left his door open all the way.

Meredith looked genuinely weirded out. "He's never done that before."

"And he might never again." Me, just trying to be helpful.

"It's always something new," Ethan said, except I couldn't tell if that was a complaint or his way of dismissing it as nothing serious.

We dawdled around, binning the idea of a second movie, and while we talked about going to bed too, by the time I trailed off to the guest room, Meredith was still up, finding one more thing, one more thing that needed doing. Between each, she would check to make sure Micah was still down for the long count.

And it *was* serious. A thing like that, you'd naturally assume it was a one-off, unique to your own four walls. But the same scenario was going on all over.

You feel guilty for not realizing that … but really, what could we have done even if we'd known?

* * *

Micah had no recollection of any of it the next day, and seemed his normal self, which is to say infused with the exuberant power of a thousand shrieking suns and ready to expend it on the nearest expanse of grass or cluster of playground equipment he could get to. He had a swimming class in there somewhere, too.

"I wouldn't worry about it," I told Meredith as, in a park a mile from their home, we watched him brachiate along a set of monkey rings, him and a couple dozen other high-decibel yard-apes. "I did a thing or two like that when we were little. I don't remember it, just Mom laughing about it."

"What did you do?" she asked.

"One night she found me sleeping on the floor at the end of my bed, on my back, butt against the bed and my legs bent at the knee so they were up on the mattress. She asked what I was doing down there, and according to her, I said: 'Oh, Mom, it's just a fad, you don't understand.'"

She shrugged, no recollection of this either. "How old were you?"

"It was a few years ago, one weekend I was home from college," I said, and Meredith rolled her eyes and kicked me lightly in the shin. "Primary school sometime, it doesn't matter."

"That was just you being your goofy self, it's not the same," she said. "Last night, that was … worrisome."

It would be to her, even though I thought she was reading more into it than there really was. Kids just did creepy things sometimes.

But I understood her being upset, just the same. I'd been sent to corners a few times, at home and at school. A couple times, in class, I'd also been ordered to stand with my nose pressed into a small circle drawn on the chalkboard. I could barely reach it, and had to strain. Both were unpleasant, shameful experiences, but the corner was worse. It was more isolating, the way the walls came together, closing in. And while the chalk circle was its own punishment, the corner was just a prelude, a holding cell where I had to wait for some more overt penalty that was coming.

The corner was a container that gradually filled with dread.

"Where did he even pick that up?" Meredith asked.

"You've never done it to him?" "Sent him to the corner?"

She shook her head no. "When he gets a time-out, it's usually just having to sit in a chair."

"What about pre-school last year? Do they do it there?"

"I don't think so. It's not on their list of approved disciplinary measures. I'll ask."

I couldn't help it: The list I instantly imagined included both the revocation of playground privileges and thumbscrews. I couldn't joke about it with her, though. She wouldn't have laughed, only glared. *That's not funny, Brook.* Not even a little? *No!* There was a time, though, and I rather missed that version of my sister. The current one was less coiffed, less blonde, and altogether more disheveled, but wound tighter.

Then again, the prior model was the one who'd

sworn she was never going to have kids, because (a) she had too much else to live for besides some parasitical offspring, and (b) kind of a crap world to bring one into anyway, wasn't it, what with rising oceans and climbing temperatures and that sense of malaise that we were all scrabbling along the downside slope of a bell curve with our parents on its apex behind us.

People change, some more drastically than others, and sometimes for reasons that aren't obvious. She hadn't even gotten pregnant by accident.

"And what does Micah think he needs to be punished for, that was the worst part," she said. "Did you see him? He looked…"

Hopeless, I thought, but didn't dare utter this either.

"Look at the way he's coming off right now. That's a boy who doesn't feel guilty for anything," I said instead. Then I pointed toward the sidelines, where one of the kids had gone sullen and tearful and bratty enough to hurl away a sandwich as soon as his mom gave it to him. "Now there's a kid who looks like he could use a little more punishment in his life."

I scanned the crop of parents, nearly all women plus one beleaguered-looking dad.

"I see you've got some hot moms here," I said. "Any hot *single* moms?"

Meredith huffed. "That's privileged information. Besides, you might want to start with hot running water at some point today."

I knocked shoulders with her. "Come on, there's got to be some MILF action you can set me up with. You don't want the sole responsibility for keeping me entertained the whole time I'm here, do you? You see how easy it is for me to have a corrupting influence on your husband."

"Let's keep that in the family, okay? I'd like to still be able to show my face here after you leave." Then she started to laugh, the thing I'd been after all along. "What was that repulsive pick-up line you used to use in college? You swore it worked a few times just because it was so pitiful."

"'Let me lower your standards' ... is that the one you're thinking about?"

"That's it." She gave me an abrupt sideways look. "Ewww, you're not still...?"

"No," I said, then gave the playground a predacious once-over. "But what better place to bring it out of retirement?"

She squared off with me, starting to loosen up. "I know you're just trying to goad me. It's like your favorite sport now or something. I know you're not half as revolting as you pretend to be."

"That's almost generous of you."

"You're actually good dad material, if you'd ever get serious and decide you want that. You really are. Every time I get to watch you with Micah, I see how true that is. You know one big reason why? You're patient. At every age he's been around you, you've been infinitely patient with him. I bet you don't even realize how important that is."

"It's probably just the weed."

"Uh huh. Probably." She sounded wholly unconvinced. I couldn't faze her anymore this morning. "Keep telling yourself that."

We quieted down and watched the kids play, but every now and then I sneaked a peek at one of the moms, imagining what life would be like with her, chaotic breakfast tables and weary dinners, never-ending laundry cycles and overbooked calendars, and always, always, this stubborn guilt that she could've been doing better instead of recognizing that maybe she was doing a pretty terrific job with what she had. It didn't sound so bad.

Now the big question: Could I elicit as much
patience as I apparently possessed?

Which steered me toward the drama with the kid
who'd flung the sandwich, to see how that was coming
along. Maybe my legendary patience had limits.

The boy was shaking his head no, no, no. I couldn't
hear what he was saying over the cacophony of shouts
and squeals, but I'd always been good at reading lips.

I don't wanna go home for a nap, he appeared to be
saying. *I don't wanna have to stand in the corner again.*

He really didn't. I'd never seen a kid more adamant
about anything.

They're mean to me there.

They're mean everywhere, I could've told him. But of
course that just would have been another evasion, the
kind I'd always been so good at, to keep from
confronting the real issue until it was too late.

* * *

That night Micah was at it again, up and in the
corner within ninety minutes of bedtime. They had him
knock back a shot of children's NyQuil in hopes it would
keep him down until morning, and this worked at least
as long as it took for the rest of us to drift off. But I later
woke in the guest room to the sound of stressed-out
crying, and knew Meredith had found him back where
he didn't belong, and when I checked my phone, found it
was 3:18 a.m.

I got up. Who needs more than three solid hours,
anyway?

"I'll watch him," I told my sister. "Just go to sleep.
I'll stay up and watch him."

In a chair in a room in the glow of a dim nightlight
watching over a little boy who made no noise as he slept
— it felt like I was the one with a problem.

As I watched Micah not move, watched his clock do

nothing, I asked myself how it was possible to get lost in a chair. The stillness of the room, and the house beyond it, seemed to deepen and grow. It was more than an absence of activity. It felt like an actual void, cut off from everything bright and warm. There were no neighbors anymore, and when a car rolled past on the street, the headlights might as well have been a flicker from another galaxy. I could no longer feel certain that Meredith and Ethan still existed anywhere I could get to from here.

And within minutes, Micah got up. One more time.

He rose with a start, as if someone had poked him awake. He pushed himself up to sit on the edge of his bed and sighed, the most bone-weary sigh I'd ever heard, then trudged over to the corner. To wait. To wait, apparently, as long as it took. I let him get there before I made a move to intercept him.

"Micah," I whispered at his ear. "What's going on?"

It took awhile for the words to sink in, like they were settling into ooze. Then he put his finger to his lips. *Shhhh.*

"They'll hear you," he whispered back.

"Who will?"

The same as the night before, he didn't answer. Now I wondered if it wasn't because he hadn't heard the question, and instead was because he really had no words for the answer.

I remembered the kid from the playground. "Are they mean there?"

"Yes," he said. "They hate everybody."

"Are they the ones that tell you to come here and wait?"

He nodded.

"What if you didn't listen to them?"

He had to let that one sink in too. Then, "They'll just make it worse."

"Let's go for a ride," I said. "Let's go camp out downstairs."

I hoisted him up against one shoulder and carried him to the family room, where I curled him onto the couch. The plan was to spoon with him and trap him in place so we both could sleep until morning. But first, I felt a need to go back upstairs to Micah's room, to stand where he'd stood, to wait where he'd waited, and just … see what was there to perceive, if anything.

I'd forgotten since childhood: You don't so much stand in a corner as lean into it, a shoulder on each wall. Your chest and the walls make a triangle, a connection like a closing circuit. I'd forgotten how the sound of your breathing comes back at you. At your feet, three planes coming together, wall and wall and floor. Overhead, the same. Except it was so dark, I couldn't see anything, definitely not at my feet.

Above, though…

Was there suddenly more light? Or were my eyes getting accustomed to what little there was? I stared at that murky, shadowed point in space where the planes met and the lines converged — x-axis, y-axis, z-axis — into the corner of a cube. It occurred to me that they didn't just stop. Each axis had to keep going on the other side of the wall and beyond the ceiling, continuing into another dimension.

Maybe that was just the weed, too.

But I could still feel it. Something more than shadows was building here. There was a sense of pressure, a warping of the space contained by the angles, the way a balloon distorts on one side when squeezed from the other.

Then I saw it, just for a moment, the convergence point bulging into a kind of circle, as if a sphere had intersected the corner of the cube, to reveal — I thought of it as an eye even before I realized it probably was one.

Not because it looked like any eye I was used to seeing, and seeing with. It wasn't. Instead, it was a multifaceted network of hexagons, a compound eye. Yet before I even realized this, I was thinking of it as an eye because it gave me the impression that, whatever it belonged to, it had seen me. Then it winked out.

I backed away, stutter-stepping, until I ran into Micah's bed and dropped butt-first onto the mattress, where I sat and watched the corner for a long time. But it only stayed a corner, pretending to be normal.

Downstairs again, I found Micah where I'd left him, and tried my best to keep him safe through the rest of the night.

It must have worked. The next thing I knew, Meredith and Ethan were standing over the family room couch as daylight scratched at the windows.

"Explain...?" she said.

"We're camping out," I told them. "Listen, you really should let Micah sleep in your bed tonight. There's something wrong with his room."

* * *

And twenty-four hours later, the next morning, it didn't matter what else we might have tried to get Micah past this strange phase, or what conclusions we might have come to after more clueless debate on what was going on with the poor kid. Because this time I woke to the sound of, well, not so much crying as keening.

While fumbling out into the hallway, I begged all the unseen forces that never listened to make whatever I might find something that would surprise me. Meredith had broken something and cut her foot. A bird had gotten in through the window and was panicking. Something small, something she was overreacting to. Anything but the obvious. Anything but Micah.

But, like I said, they never listened.

My nephew and my sister were both wearing pajamas, and she was cradling him in one corner of the bedroom … which, I had to guess, was where she found him as soon as she'd awakened a minute earlier. Ethan was a couple feet away, in a T-shirt and boxer shorts, and had dropped into a fetal squat, wrapping himself up with both arms.

To look at Micah, you wouldn't know anything was wrong. He looked like he was sleeping. But a mom would know better, wouldn't she? She'd know.

And nobody cries like that over someone who's just hard to wake up.

* * *

I stayed over, longer than I'd planned, for the funeral and another few days past that. Staying felt wrong, and I had a gaming shop that wasn't going to continue running itself for much longer, but to leave would've felt worse. Mostly I listened, because there was nothing I could say that would make anything one bit better.

Cheer up, you're not in this alone, it's on the news, this is going on all over — a lot of good that would do. But it was true. You could call it an epidemic, but it hadn't started in one place, then spread. It seemed to be going on everywhere at once, with no center, and had been for over a week before Micah succumbed to it. It merely took some time before the pieces began coming together to make the big picture, terrible as it was. Every death is local.

So during those first few days, I listened, and hugged Meredith and Ethan, a lot, because they didn't seem to have it in them to hug each other. And when I went back to Colorado, finally, that was the last time I saw them as a couple.

Statistically, the odds are pretty grim that a couple that loses a child will split up. It's not something you ask about, but I have to wonder if it doesn't come down to two-way blame and an unwillingness to forgive.

Meredith and Ethan didn't buck those odds. And I can state definitively there was blame between them, maybe not out in the open, but I'd noticed undercurrents of it in that first week after Micah was gone, each of them wondering why the other hadn't awakened when Micah squirmed out from between them to go stand in the corner for the last time. But they blamed themselves, too, and so did I, for the things I'd noticed and didn't know how to process into something meaningful, preventative.

Within a few months, Meredith went back to live with our parents for an undetermined period of time. Ethan downsized homes for obvious reasons, but it didn't matter for long. He worked as a wind turbine technician, a dangerous job even on the most upbeat day of your life, and one day he fell 200 feet to the ground. His partner on the job said he didn't scream once on the way down.

Did he do it on purpose? I don't know. But I do remember him telling me he'd decided to make a career in renewable energy not only because it couldn't be outsourced to some third-world indentured servant, but because he cared about the world Micah would be growing up in, and about leaving it a little cleaner.

I can see how something like that would stop mattering.

The world no longer looked like a place anybody would be growing up in eventually.

* * *

In the grand scheme, they were dropping all over. It was more than local, more than regional, more than national. It was global. Everywhere, parents were waking up to find their children dead in corners, for no apparent reason. Autopsies couldn't pin it down. It was as if, one

244

medical examiner said, they were being switched off.

The phenomenon was reminiscent of SIDS — Sudden Infant Death Syndrome — so somebody somewhere tagged it STODS, for Sudden Toddler Death Syndrome, and the label stuck, even though most of the casualties had already learned to walk just fine.

The cure sounded simple enough: *keep them out of the goddamn corner*. Easier said than done, though. I knew from talking with my sister that anyone who tries to watch a kid every moment of every day slips up eventually. What could you do? Tie them down to their beds? Lock them out to sleep in the yard as the seasons change and the nights turn cold?

They died anyway, and the ages got younger. They died in cribs and playpens; those have corners too. They fell asleep in cars and never woke up; angles meet in cars, as well. Desperate parents left their houses and apartments to move into tents in backyards and parks, yet this only delayed the inevitable, at least in the square and rectangular tents. Soon, you couldn't find a round, domelike tent for sale anywhere — not for retail prices, anyway. If you had the money, you could turn to the enterprising people who, loath to let a disaster go to waste, had bought them all up and were letting them go online for tens, even hundreds, on the dollar.

But whatever was outside always seemed to get in eventually. We live on a spherical world, but that's one fractal that doesn't scale down well. Across the surface, it's mostly angles.

Then there were the guardians of reason, who kept insisting at increasing volume that people were being hysterical and superstitious, that corners weren't a cause, because that was impossible. Instead, this was a quirky behavioral symptom of some fatal malady, maybe a new virus, that hadn't been identified yet.

Their children died too, no matter how thoroughly they'd been quarantined.

At least they stayed consistent after the video came out. All they had to do was call it a hoax or an optical glitch, or just hold up a contemptuously dismissive hand and say we don't know *what* it shows.

I must have seen it two hundred times. Whenever someplace ran the clip, I had to stop and see it again. It was like one of those scenes in a movie that you watch over and over, wishing for it to turn out differently. Just once.

Her name was Heather Myers, and in a matter of weeks her demise became the most viewed death since the assassination of John F. Kennedy. She was eight years old.

It was recorded with a high-definition nanny cam her parents hadn't needed to set up for years, but broke out of storage, mounted on a shelf in her room, and connected to a laptop, so they could keep an eye on her in this new plague age. The story went that they were watching her in shifts, and then one of them zonked out. So when Heather got up around 2:30 a.m., nobody was awake to intercept her.

Looking down from slightly above, the footage has that ghostly quality common to infrared. When she stirs and sits up on the bed, her hair looks white. For a couple of moments she appears to be having a conversation with someone who can't be seen, but there was never any audio, so whatever she said was lost. Then it's off to the corner with her. You never see her face again. Just her back.

Most showings of the video fast-forward through the next twenty-two minutes, because all she does is stand there. The timestamp numbers in the corner whir, and whatever small shifts she makes look tight and jerky, like she's vibrating erratically. Then the count returns to real time and you wait for the inevitable, the way she drops to the floor like a puppet whose strings have been cut.

You suspect you must've missed something, and unless you have superhuman eyes, *Matrix*-style bullet-time vision, you probably did. The prepared video backs up for a helpful slow-motion replay, frame by frame, until it freezes and you see what was over and done with in about 1/30th of a second: a pulse of energy that seems to originate in the corner over her head and zigzags down to connect with the top of her skull, like an arc from a Tesla coil. Even then, it's hard to discern, because it isn't bright, the way you expect an energy discharge to look. Just the opposite.

Black lightning, someone called it. What other name could you give it? That's exactly what it looks like.

You hope she didn't suffer, and it doesn't appear she did. The impression you get is that someone, something, somewhere, just shut her down.

That the footage was airing throughout the world every few minutes of every hour of every day might have seemed like a good idea. It's a warning. The unexpected result was how the death rate spiked higher still, parents deciding to snuff their own children, for their own good, instead of letting this happen to them.

"I'd rather send him to God pure than let the demons take him," one father said in a notorious clip. *"I'm not sorry I did it, only sorry I had to. I'd do it again."*

And so it went, as an entire generation continued to fall, one way or another.

As for the Myers, Heather's parents ... they didn't stay together either. I didn't have the heart to look up what happened to either of them after that.

But I still remembered them two years later, whenever I thought of Meredith and Ethan, deep into this quiet holocaust, while wondering why now, of all times.

Why did I have to pick now to fall in love, to be a
stepfather?

* * *

For theoretical physicists, it was the best of times, it
was the worst of times.

They got to be rock stars. Not just to an audience of
predisposed geeks, but to the general population, even
the ones who found science somehow suspect. A few had
been rock stars for years already, because they were
telegenic and had a knack for teaching, making brain-
twisting concepts accessible to anybody who didn't
drool. Now they all had a platform and the entire world
was paying attention.

Then again, in their newfound celebrity, they were
presiding over what could only be called an extinction
event. Bummer, there.

They spoke of higher dimensions and the theory that
multiple universes existed side by side, like bubbles.
They speculated that what was happening was the result
of an overlap, or a spongy collision in the foam of space-
time. They mused about what might happen when
matter and energy occupying the same space at widely
differing frequencies suddenly entrained. They went on
tangents about multidimensional geometry, and
explored the idea that physically defined lines in our
space projected into the space of someplace else, creating
pathways that could be followed back to our own. What
looked to us like a corner may have been, to them, a
crossroads.

Them...? There had to be a them, of course, even if
we had no clue who or what they were. Just that they
seemed to have no interest in sharing.

Whatever the experts disagreed on, and that was
most of it, they all agreed on one thing:

You don't need to kill off every individual or even

most of them, to exterminate a species. Just the youngest, the most vulnerable. Just the ones who embody the future. Eventually, millions of funerals later, everybody gets the message. All it takes is patience. All you have to do is wait for the rest to age and die off of whatever would've killed them anyway.

This was a long-term plan, obviously.

You don't even have to kill off all the young ones. If a few slip through, no matter. They'll grow up witnessing enough death and mourning that the last thing they want to do is breed. They'll see all they need to of the kind of pain they don't want any part of.

"I'm never having kids," Jodi would say.

She was seven years old and had never met Meredith, yet sounded exactly like my sister when she was in college, with one difference: I *believed* Jodi.

"Does it hurt to get your tubes tied?" she asked me one day.

"Do you even know what your tubes are?"

"Sure I know. Everybody knows that." She was bluffing. I adored the way she bluffed, the full-statured, how-dare-you-question-me conviction behind it. "Are *your* tubes tied?"

"I've got different kinds of tubes. You don't tie those, you have them snipped."

Jodi waited for more, then got impatient. "Well? Are they snipped?"

"Yep."

"Did it hurt?"

More than you could ever know, I thought, but that's not the answer you give a seven-year-old you're trying to keep alive day by day, and happy, even though she's already lost nearly every friend she ever had.

"Not for long," I told her instead.

She would come to me with things she wouldn't bring up with her mother — I guess because Jodi could read faces like a human lie detector, and could see there were conversations that caused her mom visible distress, while I was more utilitarian. I was the next best thing to a real father: I wasn't going away, didn't embarrass easily, and would tell her as much of the truth as I could.

Sometimes I would catch Elsa watching me with her daughter, content to let whatever was passing between us play out, and I could hear Meredith telling me what seemed ludicrous at the time: *"You're actually good dad material, if you'd ever get serious and decide you want that."*

And I wanted it after all.

It just wasn't supposed to be like this.

Jodi and I would often go for next-best-thing-to-father and daughter walks, straying from our neighborhood in one direction or another. Sometimes we'd head to a park with its silent playground, where I would push her on a swing set whose chains creaked like an old man's knees, as if it took them awhile to remember what it was like to move. For Jodi's sake, I would miss the step-cousin she'd never get to play with, and she would grill me on topics that careened between trivial and profound.

"Why do they hate kids so much?" she asked one day. "Those people on the other side, what did we ever do to them?"

"Well, for starters, they're not people," I said. "I don't think they're anything close to people."

We were scuffing along a road a few blocks from home, on the edge of things, where vacant lots and empty land bore the scars of early construction that had started a couple years ago, then stalled and never resumed. With a population in sudden, steep decline, what use was there for new homes? Actually, this time there was — architects had started to rethink everything about what a new house was supposed to look like, and what they'd come up with resembled an amoeba more than a traditional home, and I guess the developers had decided it was cheaper to start elsewhere than retrofit the boxy basements and foundations that had already been laid here. In a few places, skeletons of two-by-fours weathered where they stood.

"If they're not people," Jodi said, "then what are they?"

"I don't have a clue." No lies. "People a lot smarter than I am have gotten into fistfights trying to sort that out."

"That's dumb," she said.

"Smart people have dumb moments."

That didn't do anything for her morale, and I regretted having said it, because I feared it would linger the rest of her life. However long that proved to be.

There's a remark I encountered once: that in little boys, there's almost no hint of the men they'll become, but in every little girl you can already see the woman she'll be. And in Jodi, I really could see her future self, if she could make it there: thoughtful and confident, like her mother, but more impatient without being cruel about it, and with a crusader's sense of justice.

The latter quality was why she enjoyed walking this particular route, past the acreage where the construction had faltered. As young as she was at the time, she'd been terribly concerned about the resident prairie dogs that were slated to be gassed for living in the wrong place, and she'd gone door-to-door collecting money for their legal defense by an ecological group that wanted time to trap and relocate them.

Now, I think, she looked at their dirt-ridged mounds and their scurrying brown forms as a personal victory, even a symbol of hope. She was clever enough to look at big rodents and see civilization on the brink.

"We're like the prairie dogs were. That's why they hate us. We're in the way," she decided. "But look, *they're* still here."

And maybe they were safe from us. But they still had to watch out for hawks.

We'd turned around and were on our way back home when Jodi picked this day to ask me the worst thing she ever had.

"Do you think the black lightning hurts?"

I certainly had a parent's impulse to tell her to not worry. To make promises I had no way of keeping, and in the process deceive myself that she couldn't see straight through that. It was a daily battle.

"It doesn't seem to," I forced myself to say. "It seems quick."

"Where do we go when it hits?"

"Nowhere, if you're lucky. Nowhere at all. If you're lucky, it's like a light being switched off."

"You're supposed to tell me someplace beautiful," she smirked. "Where my friends and my dead cat are all waiting for me."

"And if your mom asks, that's exactly what I said."

Okay, so the woman Jodi would become would have a cruel streak in her after all, just for laughs.

"Race you," she said a half-block from home, and broke into a sprint.

I let her keep the lead. We had different doors we went in: the normal front door for me, and for her, I'd rigged a little round tunnel into the back that she was still young enough to find crawling through fun.

So it took her longer, and the race was a draw.

Once inside, I went through my usual obsessive-compulsive routine, inspecting all the corners and edge lines of the baseboards and molding I'd plastered thickly over, turning right-angled rooms into cave chambers where ceilings and walls and floors flowed smoothly into each other, connected by little round hobbit-style doors for Jodi to pass through. As I did every time, I tried to look at it all with fresh eyes, asking, *What did I miss, what did I miss, what could I have missed?*

This was a daily battle too.

* * *

Hope rekindled for a while. The excitement and tension were remarkably like in the movies, as the people with the big brains came up with their Hail Mary plan. The human race strikes back. Welcome to Planet Earth, motherfuckers. Don't let the lithosphere hit you in the ass on the way out.

Exactly what the plan entailed, we lowly civilians didn't know, apparently didn't need to know, but there was a good chance we wouldn't have understood even if they'd spelled out the details. So where was Jeff Goldblum in all this, I wondered. He'd break it down for the rest of us. About all we knew was that it was happening at the Fermilab Main Injector particle accelerator west of Chicago, with an end goal of keeping the great veil intact so everyone could get back to pretending we were the only things in the cosmos that mattered.

Elsa and Jodi and I made pancakes that morning, while streaming the live feed from outside the 6800-acre facility on my laptop at the kitchen table.

"This is boring," Jodi said after watching for a few minutes. "It's just some guy out talking in front of a building."

"It's all going on underground," Elsa told her. "Thirty feet down."

"Then why don't they show it down there?"

That one I fielded: "Because then it would just be some guy talking in front of a wall, and you'd think that was *super* boring."

"This way, at least there are birds," Elsa said.

She tried to keep it light. Elsa always tried to keep it light. But to me, the tension from her was as radiant as a heat lamp. She had a long body, long limbs, a long face, long hair yanked back into a ponytail, and now seemed like an assembly of taut cables, topped off with eyes wide with apprehension.

So she was already primed for catastrophe. There wasn't much change in her demeanor when, in the middle of the broadcast, the guy doing the live feed stopped in mid-nod and touched his earpiece, scowled downward a moment, and said, "Can you repeat that?" and then glanced up with eyes like Elsa's just before the video went blank and the sound went dead.

I couldn't move. Not a twitch. That feeling you get right before a chair tips back too far? Exactly. A thousand miles away, here I was waiting for a shock wave, with no idea what it would be like. If the fabric of our reality came ripping apart one colliding light-speed particle at a time, would we know it was happening?

Would I have time to tell them I loved them?

I said it anyway, just in case, and was glad I did, even if it wasn't the last time.

Over the next few hours, nobody came forward to announce what went wrong, although the helicopter footage started to appear. There was no smoking rubble to see, but since there was familiarity in that, what actually was visible seemed far worse precisely because it was so strange and *un*familiar.

Thirty feet underground, the Fermilab's Main Injector accelerator was a two-mile ring, but was now a two-mile trench of collapsed earth, like a giant moat surrounding a newborn island of green grass and thick trees. The soil continued to subside for the next fourteen hours, as if something wasn't yet done sucking it down from underneath. There was speculation of having created a vacuum of unimaginable power. There were rumors that most of the subterranean infrastructure was simply gone.

And I wondered if it was possible to slam a door shut so hard you only end up widening the doorway.

* * *

There are days you wake up and, despite your best hopes and greatest efforts, nothing's changed. The wrong people still die.

Here's how you know that everything arrayed against you, seen and unseen, has won: *I can live with this,* you tell yourself. *What's the big deal, anyway? It just takes a little getting used to.*

That, and the fact that tears no longer seem as wet, as long as they keep running from other people's eyes.

* * *

Then there are the days you wake up and everything has changed. The world around you and the world beyond and the world beyond that. My sister could tell you all about this.

Sometimes you see it coming, sometimes not. As for which is better, which is worse ... probably I should have given up ranking things as better or worse a long time ago. I just knew I recognized the sound of a brand-new now in Jodi's voice that moment we heard it:

"Mommy?" she said from the foot of the bed. "Brook?"

I started to sit up, get up, but then Elsa's hand was on my arm, holding tight and pulling me back down.

"No. I don't want to know," she said. "Not yet."

Instead, she held out her other arm, beckoning for Jodi to join us, that whatever it was could wait. We could defy it that much, by a minute or a morning, as long as we were together. So Jodi crawled onto the bed, and if she'd been my daughter for real, she would have squeezed in between us, but instead she went for Elsa's arms alone, and I held her by proxy in this flimsy, makeshift shelter of curved walls and rounded doorways that I'd always feared would never be enough.

While at the window, through the curtains — I was sneaking a peek back over my shoulder — the dawn came on with a strange light the likes of which I'd never seen, with a tapestry of shouts and sirens in the distance, and every so often the sound of soft thumps on the roof.

And since it was true that you could see in every girl the woman she would be, I hoped the reverse might hold, as well. That in every woman you could see the shade of the little girl she'd been. I looked across the inches at Elsa as she, in turn, nuzzled Jodi, stared past the swirls of hair and ear, and the strong line of her jaw, which I imagined softening, plumping … and she was there, that girl, in all her varied years and phases. I wished I'd known her then, too, back and back and back some more. I wished I could have known her all along. I wished I could've shared every dream. I wished I could have been the kind of protector who could hold off tomorrows.

Because we all still had so much growing yet to do.

Eventually we hit the point where not knowing was worse, and followed the lure of this strangely hued morning to the front windows to see how the world had changed. It was beautiful, in its way — breathtaking, even. I assumed the sky and sun were still there, but to our eyes they'd been replaced by something like the Northern Lights, only crisper and more malevolent.

The black lightning wasn't really black after all, not when there was this much of it. The luster it gave off was more of a deep lavender. It arced from branch to branch and tree to tree, as if it had found every angle made by everything that grew. It shot between the roofs of houses, from the peaks and eaves. Throughout the neighborhood the ground was littered with the bodies of birds and squirrels, and the pets that liked to roam at night, and wilder things that crept unseen — here a raccoon, there a mule deer, over there a skunk — and every now and again there came another thud on the roof as one more bird fell from a sky it was no longer fit to soar.

I wondered if Elsa saw things differently now, but now was too late. There were no guns in the house, no pills, because still, she thought suicide was a sin.

We came and went from the windows, but made no moves yet for the door, to get it over with. Because it was obvious that everything in sight that couldn't scream and die was being chipped away, reshaped, refined, faceted like diamonds in the rough.

Compound eyes would prefer it all that way, wouldn't they?

I drew them close, my girls, and skimmed their faces with my rounded fingertips — the bumps of their noses, the curves of their cheeks, the orbits of their clear brown eyes — and wondered what could be so alien that it would find such smooth contours so abhorrent.

The issue was not whether God had been a polygon all along.

The issue was what was going to happen now that He was.

As the world around us was remade in His image.

Contributors

Robert Dunbar is the author of several novels, a collection of short fiction, and a nonfiction book about the roots of the horror genre.

David Morrell is the author of First Blood, the award-winning novel in which Rambo was created. He holds a Ph. D. in American literature from Penn State and was a professor in the English department at the University of Iowa. His numerous New York Times bestsellers include the classic spy novel, The Brotherhood of the Rose, the basis for the only television mini-series to be broadcast after a Super Bowl. An Edgar and Anthony finalist as well as a Nero, Macavity and Comic-Con Inkpot winner, Morrell is the recipient of three Bram Stoker awards and the prestigious Thriller Master award from the International Thriller Writers organization. His writing book, The Successful Novelist, discusses what he has learned in his four decades as an author. His latest novels are the Victorian mystery/thrillers Murder as a Fine Art and Inspector of the Dead. David can be found at www.davidmorrell.net

Tim Curran hails from Michigan's Upper Peninsula. He is the author of the novels Skin Medicine, Hive, Dead Sea, Resurrection, Hag Night, The Devil Next Door, Long Black Coffin, Afterburn, Skull Moon, Nightcrawlers, and Biohazard. His short stories have been collected in Bone Marrow Stew and Zombie Pulp. His novellas include The Underdwelling, The Corpse King, Puppet Graveyard, Sow, Leviathan, Worm, and Blackout. His short stories have appeared in such magazines as City Slab, Flesh&Blood, Book of Dark Wisdom, and Inhuman, as well as anthologies such as Shivers IV, World War Cthulhu, Shadows over Main Street, and, In the Court of the Yellow King. His fiction has been translated into German, Japanese, and Italian. Find him on Facebook at: https://www.facebook.com/tim.curran.77

Violet LeVoit is the author of I Am Genghis Cum and I'll Fuck Anything That Moves And Stephen Hawking, both of Fungasm Press. Violet can be found at www.violetlevoit.com

Thomas Sullivan is a USA Today Best-Seller and Pulitzer Prize nominee. He has been a gambler, a "Rube Goldberg" innovator, a coach, a teacher, a city commissioner, and an All-American athlete. Having lived in a dozen countries by the time he was six, Sullivan is at home in many cultures and across the literary spectrum from mainstream to genre. The Chicago Tribune introduced him as, "…a John Barth or a John Irving, with a touch of William Gaddis and maybe a dash of Kurt Vonnegut, Jr." Over 90 publishing credits in all fiction categories, his work includes eight novels in 22 domestic and foreign editions, journalism, non-fiction and active film options. Sullivan currently lives on a lake in Maple Grove, Minnesota, writing full-time and speaking internationally in venues as diverse as the House of Literature in Oslo, Norway, and American schools and universities. His inspirational monthly newsletter (Sullygram) is available free on request. Write him at mn333mn@earthlink.net. You can find him online at www.thomassullivanauthor.com

Ray Garton has been writing novels, novellas, short stories, and essays for more than 30 years. His work spans the genres of horror, crime, suspense, and even comedy. His titles include Live Girls, Ravenous, The Loveliest Dead, Sex and Violence in Hollywood, Meds, and many others. His short stories have appeared in magazines and anthologies, and have been collected in books like Methods of Madness, Pieces of Hate, and Slivers of Bone. He has been nominated for the Bram Stoker Award and, at the 2006 World Horror Convention, he received the Grand Master of Horror Award. He lives in northern California with his wife, where he is currently at work on several projects, including a new novel. Visit his website at RayGartonOnline.com.

Gemma Files is a former film critic and teacher turned award-winning horror author Gemma Files is probably best known for her Weird Western Hexslinger Series (A Book of

Tongues, A Rope of Thorns and A Tree of Bones, all from ChiZine Publications). She has also written two collections of short fiction (Kissing Carrion and The Worm In Every Heart), two chapbooks of speculative poetry and a story cycle (We Will All Go Down Together: Stories of the Five-Family Coven), also all available from CZP. Her next novel, Experimental Film, will be out by November, 2015--from CZP, naturally. Why break the pattern?

Bracken MacLeod has worked as a martial arts teacher, a university philosophy instructor, for a children's non-profit, and as a criminal and civil trial attorney. His short fiction has appeared in various magazines and anthologies including Shotgun Honey, Sex and Murder Magazine, LampLight, Every Day Fiction, The Anthology: Year One and Year Two: Inner Demons Out, Reloaded: Both Barrels Vol. 2, Ominous Realities, The Big Adios, Widowmakers, Femme Fatale: Erotic Tales of Dangerous Women, Beat to a Pulp, Splatterpunk, and Shock Totem Magazine.

He is the author of the novel, Mountain Home, and a novella titled White Knight. He recently signed with Macmillan Entertainment to produce a new book, Stranded, which will be released by TOR.

Matt Moore is a horror and science fiction writer who believes good speculative fiction can both thrill and make you think. His short story collection Touch the Sky, Embrace the Dark was released in 2013.

His columns and short fiction have appeared in print, electronic and audio markets including On Spec, AE: The Canadian Science Fiction Review, Leading Edge, Cast Macabre, Torn Realities and the Tesseracts anthologies. He's a three-time Aurora Award finalist, Friends of the Merrill finalist, frequent panelist and presenter, Communications Director for ChiZine Publications, and Chair of the Ottawa Chiaroscuro Reading Series. Find more at mattmoorewrites.com.

Elizabeth Massie, a ninth generation Virginian, is the author of 11 horror novels, 5 collections, and more than 100 short stories, published by a wide variety of commercial houses. Her more recent novels include Hell Gate (DarkFuse) and Desper Hollow (Apex). She has won the Bram Stoker Award twice – for her novel Sineater and her novella "Stephen" – and the Scribe Award for her novelization of the third season of Showtime's original television show, The Tudors. Beth also writes historical fiction, mainstream fiction, poetry, and educational materials. In her spare time she draws zombies and hippies, knits, geocaches, presents creative writing workshops to students in public schools, and reads novels of all kinds. She hates cheese, the idea of being forced to ride a roller coaster, and arrogance. She loves chai, cozy socks, little honey bats and cats, and the beach. Elizabeth lives in the Shenandoah Valley of Virginia with her husband, illustrator Cortney Skinner.

John Everson is the Bram Stoker Award-winning author of Covenant, as well as the novels Sacrifice, The 13th, Siren and The Pumpkin Man, all originally in paperback from Dorchester/Leisure Books and now published by 47North. His sixth novel, NightWhere, an erotic horror descent into dark desire, was released by Samhain in 2012 and was a Bram Stoker Award finalist. Since then, he has published two more books with Samhain (Violet Eyes and The Family Tree) and written novelettes for The Vampire Diaries and Jonathan Maberry's V-Wars universe (Books 1 and 3). He has had several short fiction collections published of his work, including Needles & Sins, Vigilantes of Love and Cage of Bones & Other Deadly Obsessions. His fourth full-length collection, Sacrificing Virgins, will be released at the end of 2015. Over the past 20 years, his short stories have appeared in more than 75 magazines and anthologies.

For more on his obsession with jalapenos and 1970s European horror cinema, as well as information on his fiction, art and music, visit www.johneverson.com.

Chet Williamson is the author of over twenty-five books and a hundred short stories, which have appeared in The New Yorker, Playboy, The Magazine of Fantasy and Science Fiction, and many other magazines and anthologies. His fiction has been shortlisted for the MWA's Edgar Award, the World Fantasy Award, and the Bram Stoker Award, and his short story collection, Figures in Rain, received the International Horror Guild Award. Forthcoming titles this year are The Night Listener & Others (a fiction collection from PS Publishing), A Little Blue Book of Bibliomancy (a collection of fiction, plays, essays, and ephemera from Borderlands Press), and Psycho: Sanitarium (the authorized sequel to Robert Bloch's original Psycho). Most of his backlist is available from Crossroad Press in ebook format. An actor, he has narrated over thirty audiobooks by various authors, available through Audible.com. Website is www.chetwilliamson.com

Paula D. Ashe is a thirty-something writer of dark fiction who only feels comfortable writing about herself in third person. Originally from Ohio, She resides in Indiana with her wife and too many animals. Paula works as an instructor of English at a community college. She is also a PhD student in American Studies at Purdue University. Before that she earned a BA in Creative Writing and a minor in Psychology, then an MA in Composition and Rhetoric and a graduate certificate in Women's Studies, all from Wright State University. You can find her on Facebook at www.facebook.com/pauladashe and Twitter @pauladashe if you're into that sort of thing.

Brian Hodge is one of those people who always has to be making something. So far, he's made 10 novels, and is working on three more, as well as nearly 120 shorter works and 5 full-length collections. His first collection, The Convulsion Factory, was ranked by critic Stanley Wiater among the 113 best books of modern horror.

Recent and forthcoming works include In the Negative Spaces and The Weight of the Dead, both standalone novellas; Worlds of Hurt, an omnibus edition of the first four works in his Misbegotten mythos; an updated hardcover edition of Dark Advent, his early post-apocalyptic epic; and his next collection, tentatively titled The Immaculate Void.

Connect through his web site (www.brianhodge.net) or Facebook (www.facebook.com/brianhodgewriter).

www.ingramcontent.com/pod-product-compliance
Lightning Source LLC
Chambersburg PA
CBHW072213170626
46813CB00003B/915

9 780979 234675